VINTAGE SPIRITS

ANNABEL CHASE

Storm
PUBLISHING

This is a work of fiction. Names, characters, businesses, places, events and incidents are either the products of the author's imagination or used in a fictitious manner. Any resemblance to actual persons, living or dead, or actual events is purely coincidental.

Copyright © Annabel Chase, 2021, 2026

The moral right of the author has been asserted.

All rights reserved. No part of this book may be reproduced or used in any manner without the prior written permission of the copyright owner. This prohibition includes, but is not limited to, any reproduction or use for the purpose of training artificial intelligence technologies or systems.

To request permissions, contact the publisher at rights@stormpublishing.co

Ebook ISBN: 978-1-83700-203-0
Paperback ISBN: 978-1-83700-204-7

Cover design: Alexandra Allden
Cover images: Shutterstock

Published by Storm Publishing.
For further information, visit:
www.stormpublishing.co

ONE

It was the afternoon of New Year's Eve and Julie Duncan sat at the kitchen table, taking advantage of a quiet moment to order groceries for delivery. If she ordered before 5pm, she'd likely snag a coveted morning slot for January 2nd. Her mother was out of cream of tomato soup and Murphy's Law dictated that Doris would have a hankering for that specific soup if the can wasn't in the pantry.

Julie's gaze drifted to the Christmas tree in the family room as she nibbled on a frosted strawberry Pop-Tart. The tree was a gorgeous blue spruce decorated with her mother's antique ornaments and lush velvet ribbons. The tree took pride of place in front of the large windows that framed their view of the lake.

Silently, Julie counted the days until she could take down the tree. She wasn't a Scrooge exactly, but she found the holidays difficult ever since the death of her husband two and a half years ago. Greg's cancer had upended Julie's life and she still struggled with the new normal. She was fifty years old. She wasn't supposed to spend Christmas alone with her mother. Greg should be here, making his overspiced jambalaya and helping Julie cope with her mother's abrasive and overbearing personality.

"I'm surprised that mangy cat hasn't knocked the whole tree down."

Think of the devil and she shall appear.

Julie turned at the sound of her mother's voice. She'd hoped to get through this one task in peace and quiet. Doris wore what Julie referred to as her mother's uniform—a peach-colored robe and plain white slippers. The older woman leaned on a cane and Julie noticed the blue veins protruding from the skin of her hand. Had those veins always been so prominent? Julie wasn't sure.

"Peggy has been a perfect angel," Julie said. The cat joined their household in July, after the death of Julie's friend, Inga Paulsen, the founder of her weekly cocktail club. Peggy had been one of four of Inga's cats, each one named after the Schuyler sisters, made famous by *Hamilton: The Musical.*

"Don't call her an angel," her mother scoffed. "She'll think she belongs at the top of the tree and make the leap."

"She only looks at the tree. She hasn't even tried to bat an ornament."

"If she breaks one of my baubles, that'll be the last thing she ever breaks in this house."

Julie ignored the threat. If Doris truly wanted the cat gone, her mother would've forced the issue by now. When Julie first brought the cat home, Doris objected, but the cat seemed to have won her over—inasmuch as anyone could win over Der Kommissar. Each day, Peggy spent hours in bed purring beside the older woman and keeping her warm. Doris was always complaining of being cold, which was the opposite of Julie, whose menopause made certain that she was forever putting out internal fires.

"What are you doing downstairs?" Julie asked. "You know you're not supposed to use the stairs."

"I've lived this long. I'll do as I damn well please." Doris zeroed in on the remainder of the Pop-Tart in Julie's hand. "If you keep stuffing your face with junk, you'll never get married again."

Julie lowered her hand to her side, no longer interested in

finishing her treat. Her mother had a way of ruining even her guilty pleasures.

"Christmas is over now. You might as well put those presents away and not leave them in plain view of any burglars." Doris pointed to the handful of parcels under the tree.

"I don't think a burglar is interested in your new hairdryer."

"They won't know what the presents are until they've already broken in," her mother countered. "By then, it's too late."

Julie refused to indulge her mother's alarmist tendencies. "I'll do it tomorrow afternoon," she said.

"Must be nice to be a lady of leisure, living off your father's pension and my social security."

Julie gritted her teeth. The only reason Julie didn't have a regular job was because her mother required full-time care. She would've been thrilled to go somewhere else for eight hours a day if it meant a break from her mother.

"I think if you're going to insist on coming downstairs against the doctor's orders that we should move your bedroom down here."

Her mother glowered at her. "I heard you the last fifty times you suggested it. I'm not interested in a new bedroom at my age. Do you want me to wander outside in the middle of the night and catch my death?"

"You don't have dementia, Mom. You'd be fine." Even so, Julie wouldn't make the suggestion again. It was clear Doris wasn't going to budge.

Her mother peered at the computer screen. "You're ordering groceries now? You should've told me."

"Don't worry. I was going to check with you before I finished," Julie said. The main reason Julie bought groceries online was so that Doris could oversee the selection. It was too hard for the elderly woman to hobble around a store and she didn't trust Julie to buy 'the right things,' despite the fact that Julie had been in charge of shopping for years.

"Let's see what we've got so far." Doris stood so close that Julie could smell her mother's minty breath. Over the past few years, the older woman had developed a peppermint candy habit. Julie seemed to spend half her day picking up those little plastic wrappers and tossing them into the trash.

"I'm ordering more cream of tomato soup," Julie told her.

Doris skipped straight over the soup to the next item. "You've got organic milk on the list again. I told you I want normal milk. You have no idea what they're putting in the milk to make it organic."

Julie bit her tongue. She'd tried to explain the meaning of organic more times than she cared to count.

"No multigrain crackers either," her mother continued. "I've lived this long without worrying about gluten or whatever else is out there threatening to destroy civilization as we know it. I'm not going to change now."

No, she certainly wasn't.

Julie removed the organic milk and multigrain crackers from the cart. "You should sit down, Mom. You don't want to get tired from standing too long."

"I sit all day and night." Doris tapped her cane on the edge of the table. "I'm not drinking soy milk either."

"That one's for me, not for you." Julie had been trying to cut down on dairy, although she still had a weakness for cheese. At fifty years old, she noticed that certain foods affected her differently than they used to and dairy was one of them.

"If cow's milk is good enough for me, it's good enough for you."

Julie removed the soy milk before the conversation went any further. She knew if she left it in the cart, Doris would rant for half an hour about Julie's malleable mind, and how she was always susceptible to the latest fads. *Remember when you used Aqua Net by the truckload? Didn't care so much about the harmful effects of aerosol on the environment then, did you?* Julie wasn't in the mood to be frog marched down memory lane, especially when those memories would be used to shame or guilt her.

"Anything else you'd like to add?" Julie asked.

Doris leaned over her shoulder. "I think that's it. Thank goodness I came down when I did."

Julie muttered a string of curses under her breath. Thanks to years of practice, she knew exactly how low to speak if she didn't want her mother to hear her.

"Don't forget I have plans tonight," Julie said.

Doris leaned on her cane. "I don't think you told me that."

"I did." She knew it with certainty because Doris had reacted with her usual shock that Julie had a life outside these four walls. "Remember, I said I'm going out for New Year's Eve, but it's not far and I'll make sure you have everything you need before I go."

"It doesn't matter to me. I have virtual plans with the other ladies," her mother said. "We're going to play poker until the ball drops."

"Yes, I know." Doris had told her about thirty times already.

"How will I get a refill on drinks and snacks if you're not here? You don't want me hobbling downstairs on my own after a margarita. I could break a hip."

Julie rubbed her temples. "Maybe you could stick with one drink and one bowl of chips tonight."

"That's your plan, is it? To starve me into submission?"

Julie would've laughed, except she knew her mother wasn't joking. No matter how good of a daughter she tried to be, her mother seemed incapable of seeing her through anything other than a warped lens.

"I solemnly swear to make sure you have everything you need before I leave. And I won't be out late."

"It's New Year's Eve. You won't be home until after midnight."

"It'll take me fifteen minutes to get home." Which meant she'd likely be home by seventeen minutes past twelve.

"Is it a man?"

Julie flinched. "Of course not."

"Didn't think so." Her mother's cane clicked across the floor. "I think I'll sit on the deck for a bit. Make me a cup of hot water with lemon, would you?"

"Mom, it's freezing out there today. Don't sit outside."

"I'll be fine. My skin is thicker than an elephant's hide."

Julie knew there was no point in arguing with her mother. "I'll get your drink ready."

She filled the kettle and turned on the gas stovetop. While she waited for the water to boil, she debated whether to change her plans. If Doris didn't get what she wanted, she had a tendency to make life difficult for Julie in the days that followed. Julie ran through a mental list of her calendar. Was there anything on the horizon that Doris could spoil if Julie chose to go out tonight? Nothing came to mind—except the next cocktail club meeting with her friends. Julie groaned as she turned off the kettle and filled a mug with water. Julie was due to host the next meeting on Friday night, which Doris was sure to ruin if Julie was on her naughty list.

She added lemon to the hot water and hurried to deliver it to her mother before it cooled down. Doris sat on an Adirondack chair that faced the lake, appearing lost in thought. Julie set the mug on the small table beside the chair and admired the view. She'd never tire of looking at the water. It didn't matter how many years she'd lived here and how many times she'd stood in this very spot. She loved Lake Cloverleaf, even in winter when many of the trees were bare and the sky was coated in gunmetal gray. There was nowhere else she'd rather be.

"Best view in town," her mother said with an air of satisfaction.

"It really is."

Her mother glanced up at her. "Have you seen the cardinals lately?"

"No, but I haven't been watching carefully." Cardinals were her mother's favorite type of bird. She loved the way the male's red feathers stood out no matter the seasonal backdrop.

"The other day I spotted two females and a male. I bet there's a second male around. They're always in pairs."

Unlike us, Julie thought, but didn't say out loud. Never in a million years did Julie expect to become a widow in her forties. She thought she'd have Greg in her life until they were too old to pluck their own chin hairs.

"Can I make you an early dinner?" Julie asked.

"I'm not hungry," Doris said. "Besides, I want to leave plenty of room for snacks tonight."

"Good idea." Julie was grateful that she didn't have to make dinner. Cooking wasn't her specialty and meals for her mother tended to become more challenging than necessary.

Doris sipped her hot water. "Where are you going tonight?"

"Libbie is having a small party at her house."

Her mother blew a disappointed raspberry. "That piece of milquetoast? If you're going out, at least go somewhere good. Isn't Kate having a party?"

"No, Kate is going to Libbie's." Julie knew her mother was a big fan of Kate Golden.

"I guess that other one will be there, too. The little Italian."

"Rebecca. Yes, she will."

Her mother harrumphed. "Well, at least you have friends."

Amen to that, Julie thought, and retreated inside.

As much as Julie loved her friends, she found it hard to spend New Year's Eve with them. Libbie was in a new relationship with a lawyer named Ethan Townsend and radiated joy. Kate and her husband Lucas were stronger than ever. Rebecca seemed content to be single, probably because she was constantly surrounded by animals. She was like a modern-day Snow White. Julie wouldn't have been the least bit surprised to learn that woodland creatures cooked and cleaned for her.

They toasted to the new year as the clock struck midnight and exchanged hugs and kisses. Julie went through the motions with a huge smile plastered across her face, fully aware it was false cheer. Why would she want to celebrate another year without Greg? The whole 'new year, new me' concept didn't appeal to Julie at all. She didn't want anything new. She wanted her old life, the one with a wonderful husband and a bright future. Now she only looked forward to her weekly cocktail club meetings and the occasional book, although she had to admit even books weren't helping her escape lately. Ever since Greg's diagnosis, she'd returned books to the library without finishing them more times than she cared to count.

"I need to get going," Julie said, prompting disappointed groans from her friends. "I'm sorry, but you know Der Kommissar. I don't want to start off the new year on the wrong foot with her."

"You shouldn't feel bad about staying out," Kate said. "You're with her all the time. You deserve a life of your own."

"I have a life of my own," Julie said, a bit too defensively.

Rebecca regarded her over the rim of her wine glass. "Have you given any thought to that dating app I told you about?"

Julie gave an adamant shake of her head. "Hard pass. No dating apps." Ever. Julie was willing to roll with the times in most respects, but she drew the line at swiping left and right. With her luck, the habitual movement would trigger arthritis.

"The days of the setup are over," Kate said. "Believe me, if Lucas or I knew anyone worthy, we'd have arranged it by now."

Julie swallowed the last drop of wine in her glass. "You don't need to worry about me. I'm content with my life as it is."

"Greg wouldn't want you to be alone for the rest of your life," Libbie pointed out. "You're only fifty and in good health. You could live another fifty years."

Julie nearly choked at the thought of living another fifty years. It seemed ridiculous, but Libbie was right. Look at Doris. Despite the cane, she was still going strong—or at least her attitude was.

"I'm not alone. I have a fulfilling life, great friends...I don't need a man to be complete."

Libbie's cheeks colored. "Oh, I know that. I just mean..."

Julie squeezed her friend's hand. "I know what you mean, and I appreciate your concern."

"What's your mom doing tonight anyway?" Rebecca asked.

"Online poker with her friends."

Kate barked a short laugh. "Well, we know who the winner will be in that game."

"Are you kidding? My mother is incapable of a poker face."

"Oh, I know," Kate said. "I figure she'd bully the cards into forming the winning hand."

Julie laughed. "That sounds more like it."

"Do you need a lift home?" Lucas asked. "I'm the designated driver for us tonight."

Kate patted his cheek. "Yes, you are and I love you for it."

"I'm good, thanks," Julie said. "I didn't overdo it because of Doris." Otherwise she'd be trading one headache for another in the morning.

"Happy New Year, Julie," Libbie said. "I'm so glad we got to celebrate together."

"Me, too."

Julie drove home, catching a glimpse of fireworks over the lake and feeling guilty for not experiencing the same level of enthusiasm as her friends. She wanted to, but she couldn't quite muster it. Inevitably, something would remind her of Greg and she'd be back to lamenting his death and a life without him.

She entered the house to find Peggy meowing at the front door. The cat sounded distressed.

"What's the matter? Is it the fireworks?" She crouched down to stroke the cat's back. "Maybe I forgot to give you dinner." No, she was sure she'd filled the bowl before she left. Nevertheless, she walked into the kitchen to check. The water bowl was a quarter full and the drops of wet food around the bowl indicated that Julie had, in fact, fed the bottomless pit.

Peggy had followed Julie into the kitchen and was now winding her way around Julie's legs, still crying for attention.

"What is it, Peg?" The fireworks seemed to be finished now, although there was always some drunk yokel who tried to set off his own and ended up in the emergency room with missing fingers.

The cat darted from the kitchen at a dizzying rate of speed.

Okay, that was strange.

Julie gathered her wits and prepared to face her mother. Fingers crossed that Doris had enjoyed her poker night so much that she'd forgive Julie for going out. Julie would wish her a happy new year and quickly retreat to her bedroom for a fun-filled night of hot flashes and insomnia.

Peggy was waiting for her at the top of the stairs. Once Julie reached the landing, the cat ran into Doris's room. She hoped her mother didn't leave snacks where Peggy could reach them. Peggy was gluttonous enough to lick a margarita out of the glass if left unattended, as they discovered after an unfortunate incident with a rum and Coke.

Julie poked her head through the open doorway of the bedroom. The laptop was open on the bed beside her and there was an empty glass on the bedside table.

"Happy New Year, Mom. Do you want me to move the computer off the bed?"

When her mother failed to respond, Julie tiptoed closer to the bed to close the laptop and move it to the bedside table. Doris must've fallen asleep early tonight. Sometimes her mother's insomnia was worse than Julie's. It was only when Julie turned back to adjust the sheet that she noticed her mother's lips were blue.

Her palms began to sweat as she stared at her mother's motionless body. "Mom?"

Julie's fingers curled around her mother's wrist and felt for a pulse. Nothing. She bent down to check for breath. Still nothing.

"Shit," Julie whispered.

Der Kommissar was dead.

TWO

The days following her mother's death were stressful for Julie. She alternated between shock and action. She'd sit for an hour in stunned silence and then resume planning the memorial service. Around midnight on the third night, she endured a foot cramp that launched her straight out of bed and had her hopping around the floor in agony for a full five minutes. She placed her palms flat against the wall and stretched her legs behind her to try to ease the taut muscle. Her shouts must've alarmed Peggy because the cat was on the adjacent pillow when Julie finally limped back to bed. She couldn't remember when the cramps first started, but her feet and calves were routine offenders. Yoga, more water intake, and potassium had all been offered as potential fixes. Julie knew it was time to consider those options.

Somewhere between the hours of one and three, as she gazed into the darkness, it occurred to her that she hadn't slept a single night alone in the house since she was a teenager—until now. As though sensing her distress, Peggy began to purr, but the soothing sound did little to comfort her already-frayed nerves.

She closed her eyes, rolling onto her left side to try to sleep. Someone had told her it was easier to fall asleep on the left than the right for reasons she couldn't recall. At this point, her insomnia was winning by a landslide so she figured it was worth a try.

Instinctively, she reached across the bed to touch the spot where Greg used to sleep. During the past two and a half years, she tried to adjust her position and take over more of the bed, but it didn't feel right. Insomnia aside, Julie was comfortable on 'her side of the bed.'

It felt strange to be all alone in a big house. Greg was gone and now her mother was, too. None of it seemed real. Doris had been such an overwhelming presence in her life. Part of Julie felt relieved to be free of the criticism and demands—and the other part of her felt guilty for feeling relieved. Julie was fifty years old and had still walked on eggshells around her mother so as not to incur her wrath. It wasn't healthy, she knew that, but she'd managed. At a certain point, she recognized that her mother would never change and there was no reason to force a square peg into a round hole. Greg spent years trying to persuade Julie to stand up for herself and protect her boundaries. He gave up once he realized Julie had no intention of changing either.

"It won't make any difference," she'd said on more than one occasion. "It's pointless to say something. We'll only end up getting the silent treatment." 'The wall'—as Julie sometimes called it—was her mother's special brand of torture. Whenever Julie did anything that displeased her mother, Doris would react by first berating her, and then retreating into obstinate silence for days. Julie would be on edge until Doris finally spoke to her again, usually in the form of a benign request like 'bring in the mail.'

Julie flipped on her back and blew out a breath. This time, the wall was permanent. Death was the ultimate silent treatment. There would be no more tension in the house. If Julie wanted to eat cereal for dinner because she didn't feel like cooking, no one would be here to call her a helpless child. She could buy and eat any food she wanted without argument. As similar thoughts flooded her head, her body began to relax and her eyelids fluttered closed.

There were worse things than being alone.

The morning of the memorial service, Julie took her time getting out of bed. She was exhausted from another interrupted night and didn't look forward to the day ahead. Although Julie was fine interacting with a small group of close friends, a group of strangers made her uncomfortable and she always felt drained afterward. She didn't expect a big turnout for the service, though. Once you passed eighty, your social circle inevitably grew smaller.

Peggy cried for her food and Julie reluctantly peeled back the covers. She must've pulled them off and on twenty times during the night. Her body temperature switched from chilled to the bone to night sweats with surprising ease.

She fed the cat and returned upstairs to primp for the memorial service. Her stomach felt unsettled so she skipped breakfast. The phone continued to alert her to new messages, but Julie ignored the sounds as she got dressed. If she stopped to answer every message, she'd fall behind schedule and Doris would find a way to express her displeasure from beyond the grave.

Julie peeled a wax strip from her chin and stifled a yelp. The lazy part of her was tempted to stop there, but Julie couldn't host her mother's memorial service with a wispy beard. Hormones had to be the most ridiculous aspect of being human. They made you act crazy as a teenager and then they made you look crazy in middle age.

Once she was finished with hair and makeup, she took a moment to study her reflection in the bathroom mirror. Sometimes the image of the middle-aged woman didn't match the image in her head. Julie still thought of herself as young and vibrant, despite evidence to the contrary. Part of that might have been her mother's omnipresence. It was easy to feel youthful around Doris. Julie wondered whether she'd start to feel older now that she no longer had her mother at the far end of the aging yardstick.

Her final touch was adding two perfectly round pearl earrings to her earlobes. The earrings had been a gift from her mother on Julie's twenty-fifth birthday and she'd worn them for special occasions. It pained her to realize the last time she'd worn them had been for Greg's funeral. She'd have to wear them for something positive soon. Julie didn't want to start associating the earrings with sadness.

She swiped her phone off the bedside table and walked downstairs to await her guests. Peggy remained coiled on the neighboring pillow, fast asleep after inhaling her breakfast. Sniffing the air, Julie realized today was the day she normally cleaned the litter box.

"Too late now," she muttered. The last thing she needed was to smell like cat poop when greeting the mourners. Then again, it would enable her to keep her distance from relative strangers she didn't feel predisposed to hug.

Kate was the first to arrive. She set a box of liquor bottles on the kitchen island and immediately began to unpack. The stylish blonde excelled in Getting Shit Done.

"Libbie's on her way with the food," Kate said. "She said she texted to tell you."

"Oh, I turned off my phone earlier so I could focus on getting ready. I'll turn it back on now."

Kate helped Julie set up the alcohol station while they waited for Libbie to arrive. Julie was grateful to have a good friend who also happened to be an excellent chef. Libbie was bringing trays of food, including vegetarian lasagna, meatballs, and chicken cacciatore. Rebecca had volunteered to bring a cheese platter and mixed fruit.

Their phones lit up at the same time, signaling Libbie's arrival.

"Rebecca just pulled up, too," Kate said. "Perfect timing."

Rebecca was the first to enter, carrying a large bowl covered with plastic wrap.

"Do you want this in the fridge or on the table?" she asked, pausing to give Julie a kiss on the cheek.

"Might as well leave it out. People will be here in an hour."

"I think it's great that you're having the service here," Kate said.

Julie shrugged. "Nowhere else would've been good enough."

"Well, the house is certainly big enough," Rebecca said. "I need to go back for the cheese platter."

"I'll help Libbie unload the car," Kate offered.

Julie instantly felt better now that her friends had arrived. She didn't know what she'd do without their support.

The women entered the kitchen a few minutes later, laughing. Despite the solemn occasion, Libbie seemed happier than she had in years. Julie knew that was due in part to her blossoming relationship with Ethan. If anyone deserved to be in a happy, healthy relationship, it was Libbie. She'd previously been involved with a dud called Chris who everybody knew didn't deserve her. Julie was relieved when Libbie finally realized it, too.

"Thank you so much," Julie said. "You three are the best. Seriously."

Julie's stomach was in knots by the time the mourners arrived. She gave a brief speech in the family room and was more than happy to leave the heavy lifting to Reverend James. Doris had been a churchgoer until her infirmity kept her housebound. At one point in her life, she'd even served as church secretary.

After the service, Doris's friends gathered in the formal living room to commiserate and rehash the night she died.

"I can't believe she had lung cancer," Helen said. "I didn't even remember that she smoked."

"She stopped smoking about ten years ago," Esther said. "How can you not remember? She was miserable and gained all that weight."

"We didn't know about the cancer," Julie said. "She didn't have any symptoms. Apparently, it had metastasized to the bone." Julie opted to omit the part where her mother refused to see a doctor about the recent pain in her shoulder. It didn't matter now.

"I assumed she fell asleep," Helen said. "Look at us—we're

ancient. It wouldn't be the first time one of us fell asleep in the middle of a game."

Esther flicked a dismissive finger. "I can't stay up until midnight no matter how hard I try."

"Honestly, I thought she was drunk," Adelaide said. "It doesn't take much to knock us off our feet these days."

"Except she was already off her feet," Esther pointed out.

Julie set down a fresh platter of cheese on the coffee table.

"I'm surprised you decided to have this at the house, Julie," Esther continued. "I assumed we'd be going to Cloverleaf Cemetery until Helen said otherwise. I even wore my heavy coat."

"Mom's not being buried at Cloverleaf Cemetery," Julie said.

Esther frowned. "Why not? You don't have a plot?"

"We didn't want a plot," Julie replied. "She's getting cremated."

"But you can still have a plot," Esther argued. "Margot and Peter Burns were cremated and their remains are in their shared plot."

Julie didn't know how to respond. "I appreciate your input, but..."

"She told me she didn't want to be cremated," Helen interrupted with an air of judgmental confidence.

"When was this?" Adelaide asked. "If she wanted a burial, then why isn't she getting one?"

Julie felt the tension building in her body, spreading from her shoulders to her hands, which were now balled into fists. "It doesn't matter," she blurted, unable to contain her emotions. "It doesn't matter what she told you or when. She and I had our own discussion and she's going to be cremated."

Kate overheard the exchange and moved swiftly to Julie's side. "Julie is in charge of all decisions related to her mother," she said, placing her hands gently on Julie's shoulders in a show of solidarity. "If Doris told you she didn't want to be cremated after one too many margaritas, that's on her, because she told her daughter a different story."

"And you know Julie would never go against Doris's wishes," Rebecca added, edging closer to the group to defend her friend.

Julie didn't want to argue with anyone. She only wanted the service to end so she could reclaim the house.

After brief consideration, Esther nodded in agreement. "That's true. She wouldn't," the old woman murmured.

"You're a good daughter, Julie," Helen added.

Julie's shoulders relaxed. "Thank you. That's kind of you to say."

"We'd be lucky to have a daughter as wonderful as you," Adelaide chimed in. "My Gina won't even pick up the phone when I call. Always lets it go to voicemail." She clucked her tongue in apparent disapproval.

"Not many people would've put their own lives on hold and moved in to take care of an ailing parent," Kate said.

"Especially one like Doris," Rebecca said under her breath.

Julie fled the living room to check on her other guests. The beauty of hosting an older crowd was their tendency to fall asleep early. Julie was happy when the last octogenarian hobbled out the front door and left only her close friends behind.

"That was surprisingly contentious," Kate said.

Julie wiped down the table with a sponge. "Seriously. I never realized how many people had an opinion about someone else's burial plans."

"They looked so shocked when you raised your voice," Rebecca said. "To be honest, I was surprised, too."

Julie's cheeks colored. "Because it's not something I do often." Or ever. She couldn't decide whether her mother would've been proud or horrified.

"It was necessary and I was very proud of you for speaking up," Kate said, visibly annoyed. "Imagine arguing with a grieving child about their mother's final resting place."

"For the record, I'd like to remind you all that I want a wake," Julie said, polishing off a glass of pinot noir. She'd felt too uneasy to drink earlier and was more relaxed now that she'd finally enjoyed a glass of wine.

"We know," Rebecca replied, "but I think you should put it in writing to avoid anyone swooping in to declare otherwise."

Libbie poured herself another glass of wine. "Ethan would be happy to help you draft a will that included your desire for a wake. I've had him revise my will now that I have Inga's assets to pass along."

Inga's death in July had revealed a shocking secret to the four remaining women in the cocktail club—not only was Inga a registered witch, but she'd divided her magical assets between Libbie, Kate, Julie, and, Rebecca under Article III, Section 2(b) of the Witch's Covenant. It seemed the old expression 'you can't take it with you' also applied to magic and, instead of magic dying with the witches who possessed it, it was transferred like property to their chosen heirs. Initially, the friends had been skeptical about the claim—until Libbie had her first brush with magic, followed quickly by Kate.

"Maybe my mother died and passed her big mouth to me the way Inga passed her magical gifts to us," Julie joked, not that Julie had seen any evidence of any magic in her life. No, her life seemed to be one downhill development after another.

"Are you leaving your gift to Courtney?" Julie asked.

Libbie nodded. "I won't even tell Josh about it because I don't want to offend him."

"It's not your fault it only passes to females," Kate said. "I'm leaving mine to Ava. The boys will have to suck it up."

Julie and Rebecca exchanged glances. As the child-free women in the group, they'd have to designate someone other than offspring to inherit their assets, making the choice more difficult.

"I wish I knew what form my magic will take," Rebecca said. "That would help me decide who to leave it to."

"I don't think it matters," Kate said. "The way magic manifests for you won't necessarily be the way it shows up for your heir."

"That's true." Libbie rinsed her empty wine glass in the sink before placing it in the dishwasher. "Remember what Inga said. In the immortal words of The Rolling Stones…"

"You can't always get what you want," Kate interjected, smiling.

Libbie bumped Julie with her hip. "You get what you need."

"I need a vacation in the Seychelles," Julie said. "Do you think my magic will give me that?"

"Sadly, I don't think that's how it works." Kate covered the left-over trays with tinfoil.

"Do you want one of us to stay the night?" Libbie offered.

"I can do it," Rebecca said. "I don't have to be at the shelter until ten."

Julie wriggled her fingers. "Go. I'll be fine."

Libbie eyed her closely. "You don't look fine."

"I feel guilty, that's all," Julie whispered.

"About what?" Libbie asked.

"I don't know. That I didn't do enough for her. That I tried to hire someone to take care of her instead of being willing to do it myself. She was old and unwell. I knew she didn't have a lot of time left and I actively avoided her like Marie Antoinette avoided poor people."

Her friends gaped at her.

"Is this Stockholm syndrome or something?" Rebecca asked.

Kate placed an empty bottle of wine in the recycling bin. "Julie, you're being too hard on yourself."

"You're also glossing over reality," Libbie interjected. "You hired someone for part-time care and she quit after three days because Doris was too difficult for her. Face it, your mom was tough."

Libbie was right. Doris had behaved intolerably on purpose so that the woman would quit and Julie would be forced to be the only caregiver. Her mother took great pleasure in controlling Julie's life, even from her bedroom. The worst period was during Greg's illness because Julie was caring for both of them, darting from one room to the other to feed them and keep them company. She ferried them to doctor visits and picked up their prescriptions. Julie had no time for herself, not that she complained. The two most important people in her life were suffering and there was no way she'd let them down. Julie didn't know what she would've done without her friends during those dark days. They'd rallied to her side and helped with errands, grocery shopping, and cooking. She owed them a great debt.

"Is there anything else you need us to do before we go?" Libbie asked.

"You've done more than enough," Julie said, hugging her. "Thank you so much."

"I'm sorry I can't stay later, but I need to be up at the crack of dawn," Kate said. "It seems like every time I turn around, one of my kids has an event or an obligation to fulfill. They operate like mini-corporations."

Julie smiled. "Thanks. I appreciate you standing up for me earlier. I was worried I was about to be literally caned by hostile old women."

Kate embraced her. "Over my dead body."

Kate had changed in recent months. She'd always been a devoted friend with a wicked sense of humor but could be a little cold. This new Kate was warmer and more accessible. Julie didn't even realize there was room for improvement until she experienced it firsthand.

She walked her friends to the door and remained there until the last set of taillights blended into the darkness.

She was surprised when another set of lights pulled into the driveway and her friend Marcie vacated the car.

"Did you forget something?" Julie asked. Marcie had attended the service but left hours ago to attend her son's birthday dinner.

"My phone. I'm so sorry to intrude. I must've put it down somewhere and not realized."

"It's fine. The others just left." She ushered Marcie into the house. "Any idea where you left it?"

Marcie headed toward the library. "I was sitting in here with

Susan and Lisa. I remember we were sharing photos of our grandkids."

Julie spotted the phone on one of the chairs and pointed. "There it is."

Marcie scooped the phone off the chair and hugged it to her chest. "My son was so annoyed when I couldn't find it. He brought it for me for Christmas and didn't get the insurance."

"I didn't even think to clean up in this room." Julie rarely spent time in the library. She lifted a dirty plate off the end table, drawing Marcie's eye to the black book underneath.

"What's that book?" Marcie asked. "There's no writing on the cover."

Julie glanced at the book. "A blank book, like a journal. My friend left it for me as a gift when she died." She couldn't very well explain to Marcie that Inga had left her the book to someday be filled with magical recipes.

Marcie flipped to the first page. "Well, it's not totally blank."

Julie frowned. "What do you mean?"

Marcie tapped the page. "There's a recipe here."

Julie set down the plate and took the book from her friend's hands. Sure enough, there was a recipe on what had previously been a blank page. Her pulse accelerated as she studied the ingredients—mint leaves, club soda, lemon juice, and rum.

"Julie, are you okay? You look pale." Marcie winced. "What am I saying? Your mom just died. Of course you're not okay."

Julie gripped the book with both hands. "I'm fine, really. Don't feel like you need to stay."

"I'll help you clean up."

"It's basically done, but thanks for the offer." She walked Marcie to the front door, anxious to be left alone with the book.

"If you need anything, don't hesitate to call," Marcie said.

Julie waited until Marcie was settled behind the wheel before reopening the book. The recipe stared back at her. She debated whether to text her friends and tell them the exciting news, but she didn't want to make Rebecca feel bad. Thanks to this recipe,

Rebecca was now the only one with an empty book and no sign of magical assets.

Julie had been prepared to get ready for bed, but she figured she could manage one more drink. She scanned the ingredients again. There didn't seem to be much to it. In fact, the cocktail seemed tailor-made for someone as culinary-challenged as Julie, which made sense since the gift was meant to be specific to the person.

Julie gathered the ingredients, grateful that her mother had insisted on fresh mint for her tea. She mixed them in a highball glass, her heart hammering in her chest. Her hand shook as she raised the glass to her lips and she narrowly avoided spilling the liquid down the front of her dress.

"Cheers, Inga," she said, and drank every last drop.

THREE

The next morning, Julie dragged herself to the grocery store to restock the fridge after yesterday's service. It was somewhat liberating to be able to walk freely through the store instead of ordering online with her mother's watchful eye behind her.

As Julie passed the vitamin aisle, she ground to a halt and steered the cart toward it. Her friends had suggested she take potassium pills to ease the frequency of her muscle cramps. Julie had ignored their advice so far but decided to take a renewed interest in her own health and well-being. She'd lost her husband and her mother in recent years. Maybe she ought to consider those vitamins.

She scowled at the bottles on the shelf. Did they have to refer to the vitamins for middle-aged women as 'silver?' There wasn't anything silver about her, including her hair. Granted, she'd been coloring her hair for about a decade, but still. She tossed a bottle of women's multivitamins into the cart and continued on.

She arrived at the snack aisle and immediately noticed a display of multigrain crackers. By force of habit, she nearly bypassed them in favor of Saltines until a thought occurred to her.

I can get whatever I want.

Julie reached for the box of multigrain, feeling a mixture of glee and guilt. What would her mother say if she saw this small act of rebellion? Her hand hovered for an extended beat before she plucked the box from the shelf and placed it in her cart. She made sure to position it at the top next to her handbag, just in case she decided to put it back at the last second. She might even stop by the non-dairy milk section!

"I miss Twinkies," a voice said.

Julie turned to see a white-haired man in a dark suit standing beside her. He didn't have a cart or a hand basket, which was odd enough, but there was also something off about him that Julie couldn't identify. Not necessarily creepy or dangerous, just strange.

"I think Twinkies are at the far end of the aisle," she said, always obliged to be helpful.

He glanced forlornly in that direction. "Oh, I know. I just can't have them."

Julie smiled. "Trust me. I know how you feel."

He fixed his blue eyes on her. "Yes, I thought you might."

Julie wasn't sure whether to be offended by the comment. She didn't consider herself fat. It was more that her bones benefited from a protective layer of soft flesh.

She pushed her cart forward and felt the man's presence behind her as she turned down the next aisle. It wouldn't have seemed strange if he was actually shopping, but he only seemed to be gazing longingly at the shelves as he shadowed her. By the time she reached the bread aisle, Julie's heartbeat was like a winning slot machine. The man still followed without a single item from the store. She glanced around for an employee or even another customer, but the store was relatively quiet at this hour.

Finally, she turned around and positioned her cart between them as a buffer. "Why are you following me?" she demanded.

"I thought you might be able to help me."

"I told you where the Twinkies are."

His brow creased. "I don't need you to help me with Twinkies. I need you to help me with my son."

His son? Julie was thoroughly confused. "Is your son lost? If you speak to customer service, they can do an announcement." He seemed awfully old to have a young son, but it wasn't out of the realm of possibility. After all, Cary Grant was sixty-two when his daughter was born.

"You don't seem to understand..." The man stepped forward and it was then that Julie realized what was so odd about him. He didn't step so much as glide. Her gaze dropped to his shiny black shoes that hovered about half an inch off the floor.

The man was *floating*.

Julie backed into the shelves and nearly toppled loaves of bread in the process. "How are you doing that?"

The man looked down at the floor. "I don't know. I feel like I'm walking normally, but I don't actually feel the floor beneath my feet."

Okay, this was getting bizarre. She seemed to be alone with a floating man. Why had Julie chosen such a quiet time to shop?

"Excuse me. I need to finish my shopping," she mumbled and gripped the handle of the cart.

"Please don't walk away," he said. "You're my only hope."

A *Star Wars* reference. Greg's favorite movies. Instinctively, Julie's grip loosened. "Only hope for what?"

"To communicate with the living."

That did it. Someone was either punking her or she was officially losing her marbles. "You're telling me you're dead?"

"Heart attack," he said.

Julie stared intently at the man in the suit. He didn't seem to be pranking her, which left her sanity in question. "You're a ghost?"

"Yes. I was drawn here."

Julie looked around, perplexed. "To the grocery store?" That seemed like an odd place to haunt.

"No," he said, "to you."

To her.

Julie tried to maintain her composure as she let his answer sink in. "This has to be a joke." If she could see ghosts, why not someone she knew? Why not her mother or her husband? Even her father would make more sense than this stranger in a suit.

"Hold on. I'll prove it to you," he said.

A shopper rounded the corner and stopped her cart in front of the English muffins. The man unbuttoned his suit jacket and pirouetted his way over to her. He looked ridiculous, prancing around her, yet there was no reaction from the woman. She selected a package of English muffins and continued toward Julie. The man in the suit raced in front of her cart and she pushed it straight through him.

Julie's heart seemed to stop and she closed her eyes, unwilling to see more.

"Will you help me now?"

Slowly, she opened her eyes. He stood directly in front of her now. "What's happening to me?" she whispered.

"My son isn't aware of me," he continued, seemingly oblivious to her reaction. "I need to talk to him."

"I'm having a nervous breakdown," Julie said to herself. It was no wonder. She'd suffered two major losses. She thought she'd been holding herself together, but maybe he was a sign of the first crack in her armor.

Muttering to herself, Julie blew past him and headed for the checkout line. She needed to go home and have a nap. The stress of her mother's death was clearly having an impact on her.

"What's your name?" he asked, as Julie unloaded her groceries onto the conveyer belt. "I'm Tom."

Julie ignored him. Maybe if she refused to answer, he'd disappear.

The cashier held up the box of multigrain crackers. "I need a price check. They're not ringing up."

Julie waved a hand. "It's fine. I don't need them." It was guilt over the crackers. That's what triggered this panic attack—or whatever this was.

The cashier seemed to sense Julie's distress because she helped pack the bags and hurried through the transaction.

"Have a nice day," the cashier said, giving Julie a look that suggested she knew it was unlikely.

"Thank you." Julie practically ran out of the grocery store, nearly knocking the cart into a Valentine's Day display on the way out. She didn't want to think of Valentine's Day either because that made her think of Greg. Every year, he bought her a *Star Wars* card, like the ones children gave to each other at school. Well, every year until he died.

Tears stung her eyes as she tossed the bags into the trunk. Although Tom was out of her peripheral vision, she felt his presence nearby and it made the hair on the back of her neck stand on end.

"I didn't buy the crackers!" she shouted at no one in particular. She ducked into the car and gasped when Tom appeared next to the driver's side door.

"I could really use your help," he said.

Her heart thumping, Julie slammed the car door shut and hoped he didn't suddenly appear in the passenger seat. Her hands trembled as she started the car and peeled out of the parking lot. On the drive home, she blasted the radio to drown out the sound of Tom's voice in her head.

I could really use your help.

No, Julie thought. *I'm clearly the one who needs help.*

Julie arrived home and popped the trunk. As much as she wanted to carry more than two bags at a time to reduce the number of trips, she knew wasn't capable of it. The last time she tried to lug three bags at once, she ended up with a cramp so deep in her chest that she couldn't breathe.

"Ooh, I love Pop-Tarts," a voice said.

Julie clutched her chest and swore. "People really need to stop sneaking up on me." She turned to look at the elderly woman, who appeared vaguely familiar. Her silver hair was a bit mussed and her face was covered in liver spots. "We've met before."

"At Rebecca's shelter. I'm Rosie."

Julie snapped her fingers. "Right." Rebecca worked at a local animal shelter and Julie sometimes dropped by to chat when she was downtown.

"I adopted my sweet Mollie from there," Rosie said. "That's why I'm here, in fact."

Julie stared at the woman blankly. She'd come to talk to Julie about a dog she'd adopted from Rebecca's shelter? Upon closer inspection, Julie realized that wasn't the only strange thing about Rosie. The elderly woman was wearing a hospital gown beneath her white robe, as well as tight white socks that went up to her knobby knees.

"I don't understand," Julie said.

"I need you to talk to Mollie for me," the elderly woman said. "Tell her everything's going to be okay."

Julie frowned. Rosie seemed to have mistaken her for some kind of dog whisperer. "You should really talk to Rebecca about anything animal related. I have a cat, but that's a recent adoption and I'm still not quite sure if I'm doing everything right."

Rosie's lips parted to reveal a set of coffee-stained teeth. "If you're giving that cat love and attention, then you're doing everything right, my dear."

"Rosie, I hate to ask this, but should you be wandering around like this? Do you need me to drive you somewhere? Maybe back to the hospital?"

"Oh no. I left there a few days ago. I'm not going back."

Julie balked. Had this old woman been roaming around town in a hospital gown for days? There were plenty of cases where senior citizens with dementia or Alzheimer's went missing. Maybe people were searching for her. She pulled out her phone and texted Rebecca. If she could keep talking to Rosie, maybe the old woman would stick around until someone came to collect her.

> Rosie is at my house and wants me to talk to her dog, Mollie.

She added a crazy-faced emoji for good measure.

I don't think you mean Rosie. Is it Janice? Her dog is Millie.

No, it's definitely Rosie.

No, it's definitely not. Rosie died the day after Christmas. Complications from surgery.

The phone slid from Julie's hand and fell to the grass with a soft thud. "This isn't real," she whispered. It was another hallucination like the man in the suit. It had to be.

"Oh, my. I seem to have upset you. That wasn't my intention. I was under the impression you were a messenger."

"A messenger?" Julie repeated, retrieving her phone from the ground.

"Yes, a helper. I felt something tugging me here, so I went with it."

Julie's chest tightened and she started to worry she'd pass out and die from hypothermia in her own yard. In heaven, Doris would tell her it was her own fault for going outside without a coat, even though it was the kind of thing Doris did when she was in the mood to be difficult.

"I'm sorry. I think you have me confused with someone else," Julie said, uncertain what to do. You weren't supposed to argue with a hallucination, were you? That seemed worse somehow.

Rosie looked her up and down. "No, it's definitely you. I can feel it."

Julie didn't feel anything except ready to hurl. This woman was either a hallucination or a lunatic, and neither option was preferable.

"Are you sure your name is Rosie?" Julie asked.

The old woman looked at her askance. "Just because I have more age spots than a dot-to-dot doesn't mean I've forgotten my own name."

"I'm sorry, but I really need to unpack these groceries. Is there someone I can call for you? Or maybe I can drive you somewhere when I'm finished unloading the car?"

Rosie's lips formed a pout. "Well, this was a pointless trip. I got better service at McDonald's." She gave Julie a disgruntled look before turning away in a huff.

Julie lifted two bags out of the trunk and carried them inside, her heartbeat thundering between her ears. She clearly needed a hot bath and a stiff drink—maybe even at the same time.

FOUR

The close encounters of the weird kind had unnerved her. After putting away the groceries, Julie decided to keep her mind and body occupied by tackling an important task—packing up her mother's bedroom. She wouldn't finish in one day, but it seemed like a worthwhile project to start.

She had a few garment boxes that she hadn't used for Greg's clothes, as well as a pack of flat boxes she bought in the local hardware store. She'd always accused Greg of being a clothes horse, but it was only when she packed up his closet that she realized she'd been mistaken. Then, of course, she felt guilty for ever accusing him of buying too many clothes. Sometimes she felt like she couldn't breathe, she was buried under so many layers of guilt.

Carrying an armful of empty boxes, Julie entered the large bedroom and was immediately assaulted by her mother's floral scent. Doris had a fondness for sickly sweet perfumes that turned Julie's stomach. She dropped the boxes on the floor and crossed the room to open the bay windows and air out the room. She wouldn't be able to stay in the room for very long if she didn't eliminate the smell. A wave of heat melted through her body as the cold air hit. It wasn't often that hot flashes were helpful. Julie took it as a good omen.

She opted to start with the closet because the least-used items were kept there. It wasn't Julie's first experience with packing up another person's life and reducing it to a pile of nondescript boxes. Although Julie found the exercise depressing, she was grateful for the distraction. Anything to help her forget the bewildering incident in the grocery store and the woman in the hospital gown. She debated texting her friends about it, but she'd leaned on them enough. It was only the start of the new year and she'd already drained her reservoir of goodwill.

Julie pulled down items from the top shelf. She was tall enough to reach without a stepladder, which was convenient for the task. The first thing she found was a shoebox filled with pennies. The box was heavier than she expected and she nearly dropped it on the floor as a result.

"Pennies from heaven," she said, when she took off the lid to see what was clinking inside.

She had no clue why her mother had kept all these pennies. It didn't seem like a very Doris thing to do. She examined a few of the coins to see whether they were rare or special in some way, but they appeared to be run-of-the-mill pennies.

At the back of the shelf, Julie discovered an ashtray she'd made for her mother in elementary school. The form was misshapen and the color was a strange blend of purple and pink, but Julie had been proud of her creation. She smiled at the relic. There was no way children made ashtrays anymore. Her smile faded as she realized if Doris hadn't been a smoker, she wouldn't have died from lung cancer. As her dearly departed friend Inga would say, though —everyone has to die of something. And Doris managed to live a long time for a woman who regularly eschewed the advice of doctors because they 'smelled funny' or were 'too short.' Doris didn't even try to drum up a credible reason to ignore them.

Julie's stomach rumbled and she considered stopping to eat, but she chose to plow ahead instead. She'd reward herself with a brownie after dinner for all her hard labor.

"Meow."

Julie twisted to see the cat rubbing against one of the boxes. "Hey, Peggy. Please don't jump into any boxes. I don't need to go through what Kate did with Cat-Cat."

Cat-Cat had wandered into a box spring that was then hauled away to an incinerator. Thankfully, the cat was discovered and rescued before the situation could take a tragic turn.

Julie spotted her mother's cane in the corner of the room. She would donate it to a local nursing home, along with any other useful items she found.

She observed Peggy as the cat sniffed the neat row of shoes. Julie marveled at the similarity between each pair. Doris basically owned the same pair of shoes in varying shades of beige. How had Julie never noticed that before? As reserved as Julie was, her wardrobe choices were far more daring, which sometimes provoked criticism from her mother. Then again, everything Julie said or did seemed to provoke criticism from Doris. On more than one occasion, Julie had even been accused of breathing wrong. In her darker moments, Julie wondered whether her father's early death had been a means of escape. She wouldn't have blamed him. He'd been a quiet man who didn't express his feelings. He liked to watch golf tournaments. That was the most significant thing Julie could say about him.

Her phone lit up with a text from Libbie.

Need help with anything?

There was no way Julie would ask her friends to help pack up her mother's bedroom. The task was too personal.

No thanks.

Bringing over dinner and wine later. Will leave on porch unless you want company.

Julie smiled at the text. Libbie was a good friend.

Not sure yet. I'll let you know.

She suspected she might be too tired later to be good company for anyone, even herself.

After two hours of packing, Julie's arm muscles were sore and she had a kink in her neck. She'd had the same experience after packing up her husband's belongings, although Doris seemed to have amassed more random items than Greg. She'd kept a few of his possessions for sentimental reasons, including the Christmas suit he liked to don each year on Christmas day. It wasn't a traditional Santa suit—oh no, that was much too dull for Greg. His garish suit was covered in a design of red, green, and yellow lightbulbs and an array of ornaments, as though he was a Christmas tree. The sight of the ridiculous suit brought joy to her heart every time she looked at it.

She wished Doris had a Christmas suit or something so wonderfully silly that Julie could keep as a treasure. That wasn't her mother's style, though. In fact, Doris had hated Greg's Christmas suit and refused to take any photos of him wearing it because she thought it was 'embarrassing and juvenile.'

Pushing the negative memory aside, Julie continued with her project until she felt nauseous from hunger. Only then did she carry a packed box downstairs and allow herself to eat.

Standing at the sink, Julie heard the sound of the front door open and close. "Hello? Libbie?"

For a heart-stopping second, her mind skipped to her earlier hallucinations, but she immediately dismissed the thought. Those bizarre incidents had been triggered by grief, plain and simple.

"Hello?" Julie called again. She remained rooted in place, unable to move from the sink. If an intruder was about to kill her, the best she could do from her current position was splash them with water.

"Hey, Jules. Did I scare you?"

A familiar figure swaggered into the kitchen, and Julie's tension only intensified at the sight of him. She hadn't seen Brad in years.

His brown hair was a bit shaggier and the lines across his brow were deeper, but there was no mistaking her older brother.

"Brad," she said, her voice barely audible.

"Surprise." He waved his hands and grinned at her.

Brad moved to Phoenix more than twenty years ago and they were lucky if they received a birthday card from him. The last time Julie saw him was at their father's funeral. He'd missed Greg's funeral due to an alleged scheduling conflict. Julie would've been upset, except she'd come to accept that Brad didn't care about them.

"I didn't know you were coming," she said, although what she really wanted to say was 'you should've knocked.'

"Our mom died," Brad said. "Why wouldn't I come?"

A dozen answers flooded Julie's brain. Because you didn't care? Because you ignored her for years so why bother to show up now? Because you're a prick?

Instead, she replied with, "She died peacefully, in case you were wondering."

He nodded. "Peaceful isn't a word I'd associate with her, but okay."

Standing in the kitchen alone with her brother, Julie felt incredibly awkward. What did you say to someone you shared a house with for sixteen years but never really knew? She shifted into hostess mode. "Can I get you something to eat or drink?"

"Don't suppose you have any beer."

"As a matter of fact, I do. It's left over from the memorial service."

"Guess I missed all the fun."

"I would've told you if I'd known how to reach you." She opened the refrigerator and chose the cheapest bottle she saw. Brad didn't deserve a quality IPA. "How did you know she died?"

"Her lawyer found me."

Naturally. "I haven't gotten around to the will yet." She popped off the lid and handed him the bottle.

"Good thing I made it in time then." He took a long drink and smacked his lips, satisfied. "We should schedule a meeting with the lawyer right away. Might as well get it over with."

Julie leaned her hip against the counter. "And then you'll go home?" *To whatever rock you emerged from?*

"Depends on the will, I guess." He glanced toward the ceiling. "Should I stay in Mom's room while I'm here?"

Julie balked. He actually planned to stay in the house with her? He couldn't possibly be serious.

"You might be more comfortable in one of the local inns or a boutique hotel."

Brad downed his beer and looked at her. "Why would I stay in a hotel when my family home has plenty of space?"

"I'm in the middle of packing up her room and it's a mess."

"Then what about one of the guest rooms?" His mouth twitched. "Oh, I get it. Jules has herself a boyfriend and she wants the place to herself. It's about time, sis. Your husband's been dead how many years now?"

It took all her strength not to chuck a beer bottle at his head. "I don't have a boyfriend. I just thought you'd prefer privacy. I'll be having friends in and out..."

His brow lifted. "Good-looking friends?"

Julie noticed he didn't ask whether they were single. It was unlikely he cared about marital status.

"I have a lot of work to do in the house with Mom's things, so I think it makes sense for you to stay somewhere else. A friend of mine owns the Gaslamp. It's a motel on the outskirts of town. I can get you a good rate." She remembered a detail that might persuade him. "It's next door to Palmetto Bar."

"That old bar is still going?" He nodded, appearing to warm to the idea. "Sounds like a plan. While I'm here, why don't we call the lawyer now and make an appointment?"

Julie had no reason to object. She listened as he made arrangements with the lawyer for a meeting at ten o'clock the next morning. It sounded as though the lawyer had tried to schedule it for later in the week, but Brad seemed to be in a hurry and pushed until he got an earlier appointment. As she listened to his side of the conversation, Julie realized his voice sounded very much like their father's, except her father's had lacked the undercurrent of aggression.

Brad finished the call and slid his phone into his back pocket. "See? Easy-peasy."

"Thanks for taking care of that," Julie said.

"I think I'll take a ride over to the Gaslamp and see about a room if you want to make that call to your friend."

Julie nodded. "I'll do it right now." Anything to get rid of him sooner rather than later. His sudden appearance had put her on edge. They hadn't been close as kids and they certainly weren't close now.

As soon as he left, Julie felt desperate to take a shower. Brad had always radiated a sleazy vibe and it was clear nothing had changed on that front.

It was an unusually warm and sunny winter's afternoon, so Julie decided to take full advantage and assess the state of the garden in the remaining hour of daylight. Anything to help distract from her mother's death and Brad's unexpected arrival. Plants were not Julie's thing—she couldn't even keep a cactus alive—but she felt compelled to make sure no aspect of the home fell below her mother's exacting standards. She also didn't want to give her brother any reason to gripe, not that he had any right to complain after all these years.

She pondered the plants for about five seconds before giving up. As far as she was concerned, they all looked like weeds that needed to be ripped out. There was no way she would be able to figure out what they were or what to do with them, especially this time of year when everything looked on the verge of death.

Julie tugged her phone from her back pocket and called Libbie. Her friend's garden had become an enviable outdoor paradise in a short period of time and Julie hoped to replicate Libbie's success.

"Hey," Julie said. "Do you have a minute?"

"Of course. What's up?"

"Can we FaceTime? I'm outside and I need your expertise with the garden."

"I can do you one better. I'm already in my car about five minutes away with your dinner."

Julie suppressed a smile. "Is it Mexican skillet?"

"You know it. I made it with extra sweet potatoes for my sweet friend."

"You're the best. See you in five." Julie hung up and tucked away her phone. A cold breeze blew past her and she zipped her hoodie to stave off the chill. One good thing about menopause was that she rarely needed a heavy winter coat. Even the hoodie would overheat her if she wore it long enough.

"Excuse me, can you help me?"

Julie turned and gasped at the sight of an unfamiliar blonde standing in the yard. She looked about forty-five and wore a kimono-style robe and bunny slippers. Where had she come from? And more importantly—bunny slippers?

The woman offered a reassuring smile. "Sorry, I didn't mean to startle you."

"How are you not freezing?" Julie asked.

The woman glanced down at her attire. "Oh, ha! I didn't even notice."

"I'm not judging the outfit," Julie lied. "It just looks cold." She was totally judging the slippers, though. "To be fair, I spent weeks in pajamas after my husband died."

"Hmm. I suppose it makes sense."

"What does?"

The woman met Julie's gaze. "That I would be wearing the clothes I died in."

Julie sucked in a breath. Not another hallucination.

"I can see I've scared you," the woman said. "I'm so sorry. I was drawn here and I thought you could help me."

A lump formed in Julie's throat. Another one in need of help.

"My name is Barbara," she continued. "I live over on Sycamore Road, at least I used to. My husband is still there and..."

Julie was officially losing her mind. She clamped her hands over her ears and closed her eyes, willing the hallucination to end. Maybe if she counted to ten and opened her eyes again, the vision would be gone.

One, two, three...

She felt a tap on her shoulder and screamed.

"Oh, shit. Julie, I'm sorry." It was Libbie's voice.

Julie whirled around to face her friend. "Thank God." She threw her arms around Libbie's neck and hugged her.

"What's going on?" Libbie asked.

"Nothing." Julie waited for her heartbeat to calm before releasing her friend. "You caught me off-guard, that's all."

Libbie eyed her closely. "Are you sure that's it? You know you can tell me anything."

Julie knew, but she felt too disoriented to share. Between Brad showing up out of the blue and these strange sightings, Julie was off-kilter.

She peered over her shoulder to see whether Barbara was still there. Thankfully, there was no sign of her.

"Where's the Mexican skillet?" Julie asked, in an effort to steer the conversation to safer territory.

"On your kitchen counter." Libbie turned to inspect the plants. "Ah, I see what you mean about the garden."

"Can you help? I have no idea what I'm dealing with and I don't want to kill everything."

"No kidding. The last thing you need is Doris coming back to haunt you."

Nausea rolled over Julie at the thought of her mother returning as a ghost. She wished Libbie hadn't put the idea in her head. Now her hallucinations would probably include Der Kommissar complaining about the incorrect placement of her ceramic cherub collection.

"What's wrong, Jules?" Libbie asked. "You look pale."

"I need to pack up my mother's ceramic cherubs," she blurted.

Libbie cocked her head. "Don't try to do everything all at once. There's no rush." She shifted her attention back to the garden. "Why don't we start here and worry about the fat baby angels later?"

Julie nodded, although she thought the sooner the cherubs were packed away, the better. The last thing she wanted was to hallucinate that fat baby angels were talking to her. It didn't help that the figurines were mostly naked.

"I don't know what any of these plants are," Julie said. "And they all look close to death."

"Well, that's because it's January," Libbie explained patiently. "It's good that you're paying attention to them, though. You'll want to keep notes so you know what to do when spring rolls around."

"If there are any changes you'd recommend, I'm open to that, too, especially if it makes maintenance easier for me."

Libbie broke into a smile. "I thought you'd never ask. I have so many ideas now that I've expanded my own garden." Her gaze slid to the lake. "And let's face it, you've got the best property of the four of us."

"These days I'm looking forward to a good snowfall. The lake always looks so magical afterward."

"Speaking of magical, are you ready to taste my Mexican skillet? I added a couple new spices and I want an expert opinion."

"Then you've come to the right house, my friend." Julie was more than happy to taste test one of Libbie's dishes. Libbie was a fabulous chef and Julie loved to eat—it was a win-win for both women.

She accompanied Libbie inside, sparing one last glance over her shoulder for Barbara in the bunny slippers.

There was no one there.

FIVE

Julie tapped her foot to the tune of "Like A Virgin" as she and Brad waited to be called into the lawyer's office. The moment Brad commented on the secretary's cleavage, Julie put in her earbuds to block any additional attempts at conversation.

She was relieved when Howard Moskowitz finally summoned them into his office. Howard was short and squat with a head of thinning hair. His plaid wool suit wasn't doing him any favors either. The pattern only seemed to make him appear wider than he actually was. The faint stench of cigar smoke lingered in the air, triggering a childhood memory of her father's collection of cigar boxes, which Julie had used as storage for her Barbie accessories.

Howard shook their hands and motioned for them to sit. "Thank you both for coming. It's nice to finally put names to faces. Your mother had nothing but good things to say about you."

Brad snorted. "I highly doubt it."

For once, Julie didn't disagree with her brother.

"This shouldn't take long since we made sure that everything in her estate falls under the will," Howard said.

"Isn't that bad?" Brad asked. "I thought probate took forever."

Julie cut a quick glance at her brother. It sounded like someone had been doing a little legal research on the internet.

"Not in Pennsylvania," Howard said. "It's pretty straightforward here." He flipped open a file. "Do you want the long version or the short version?"

"Short," Brad said, before Julie had a chance to answer.

Howard scanned the document. "Brad, you're named first in the will. Your mother left you the sum of twenty thousand dollars."

Brad slouched in the chair with a satisfied smirk.

"And the remainder of the estate has been left to Julie."

It took a moment for his words to register. "Wait," Julie said. "The remainder of the estate means everything else."

"That is correct," Howard said. "Twenty thousand comes off the top for Brad and then whatever's left belongs to you."

Brad straightened. "No, that can't be right. What about the house?"

"The house is part of 'everything else.' It goes to Julie," Howard said.

"That's not fair," Brad sputtered. "That's our family home and I'm family."

"Your mother felt that it was appropriate, given that Julie and her husband sold their own house to move in and care for her when they could've made a different choice." Howard maintained a calm demeanor, leaving Julie to wonder how many times he'd had to deliver unexpected and disappointing news to relatives.

Brad's fingers tightened around the arms of the chair. "Of course they moved into that house. It's much nicer than anything they could've bought on their own."

Julie flinched at his angry and bitter tone.

"Be that as it may," Howard said, "this was your mother's reasoning."

Brad leaned forward to peer at the document. "Where did she write that part?"

"It's not written explicitly in the will, but we had several conversations about her feelings on the subject."

"If it's not written in the will, then it doesn't count, right?" Brad asked. His voice seemed to have gone up an octave.

Howard slotted his fingers together. "The part where Julie inherits the remainder of the estate is included in the will and that's what's important."

"This is an outrage," Brad said. "She only had two kids. She should've split everything in half."

Howard tapped the document. "She didn't leave you empty-handed."

Seriously. Twenty thousand dollars was nothing to sneeze at as far as Julie was concerned. In fact, it might be all the cash in the accounts, leaving Julie with a house she couldn't afford and no money. She'd cross that bridge later.

Brad jerked his head toward her. "You did this, didn't you? I bet you bad-mouthed me at every opportunity to worm your way into her good graces."

Julie certainly didn't need to say anything about Brad to make him look bad. He managed to do that all by himself.

"I didn't know what Mom was planning," Julie said truthfully. They only talked about money occasionally, usually when the older woman was berating Julie for a purchase she deemed foolish for reasons that only made sense to Doris.

"Your sister did not take part in any of our meetings," Howard confirmed. "Doris made a point of being driven here by a friend of hers so that Julie wasn't privy to the information."

"Which friend?" Brad demanded.

"I believe her name was Esther."

"Yes, Esther and my mother were good friends," Julie said. Not that Brad would know. He hadn't been a part of their lives for decades.

Instead of placating her brother, the lawyer's words only seemed to fuel his anger. Brad shot to his feet and marched out of the office without another word.

Howard glanced at the doorway. "Stomping off in a huff won't change the contents of the will."

Julie didn't bother to disguise her smile. "I'm sure you'll hear from him when he's cooled off and ready to claim the money."

She had no doubt that money was the only reason he was in town.

"You should know that your mother was very proud of you, Julie. She sang your praises at every meeting."

"Thank you," she said, although she had to believe he was only being polite. Her mother didn't sing anyone's praises.

"Best of luck with the house. It's a stunning property. You're a fortunate woman."

It wasn't often that anyone told Julie she was fortunate, not with her track record in life. Maybe her luck was finally starting to turn.

Julie was relieved that she and her brother had driven separately. She wouldn't have been able to breathe the same air as him after his outburst in the lawyer's office. Plus, she was still reeling from the outcome of the meeting. Her mother left her everything, minus twenty thousand dollars.

The house was hers.

Julie didn't realize what a relief the news was until now. She'd been harboring feelings of fear, which probably explained her recent experiences. They'd likely been projections of her fear. Julie didn't want to leave the house behind with all its cherished memories. If her mother had left half to Brad, Julie would've been forced to sell. She couldn't afford to buy him out. At this point, she wasn't even sure she could afford to keep the house, but at least the option was on the table.

Her phone rang as she pulled into the driveway and Kate's name appeared on the screen. "Hey, there," Julie said.

"How'd it go?"

"Good and bad." She exited the car and walked toward the house with Kate on speaker.

"These things are never easy."

"Brad is ready to kill me." She told Kate about the contents of the will.

"Oh, wow. I mean, I'm glad Doris came through for you in the end, but I don't envy you dealing with a twatwaffle like Brad."

"You should've seen his face. It was redder than Janine Farrell's lipstick."

Kate laughed. "I'm glad you're keeping a sense of humor about it."

"I don't feel like I have a choice. It's laugh or fall apart."

"Are we still on for tonight?" Kate asked. "If you don't feel up to it, we understand."

"No, I'm definitely in. I could use the distraction."

"I thought so. In that case, we'll be at your house at seven. Don't prepare anything. We're bringing the drinks and nibbles."

Julie didn't argue. She needed the pampering and she knew it. "Great. See you then."

As she entered the house, she spotted the cat on the windowsill in the formal dining room. It was the most neglected room in the house, but her mother had insisted on preserving it like it was a national landmark.

"You should hear about my day, Peggy," Julie told the cat. "You're not going to believe it."

Peggy meowed but declined to move from the windowsill.

"I'm having friends over later. You'll be in your element." For a solitary animal, Peggy seemed to enjoy the company of others. She especially seemed to like the members of the cocktail club, which came as no surprise to Julie. After all, they were her favorite people, too.

As Julie made her way to the kitchen, she noticed aspects of the house with fresh eyes. The crown molding. The chair rail. The hardwood floors. All hers.

"I can't believe it," she said. "It's *my* house."

"Me neither. I thought for sure she'd kick you to the curb with one of her beige shoes after she died."

Julie's veins turned to ice and she stopped mid-step. "I'm imagining things again. That's all. My mind is playing tricks on me."

"At least you're imagining me. If it were some other guy, I'd be insulted."

Slowly, Julie turned toward the sound of his voice. Greg hovered in the doorway that separated the living room from the foyer.

Greg, her dead husband.

Her throat went dry and she opened her mouth to speak, but no sound came out.

His eyes danced with amusement. "What's wrong? Cat got your tongue? Do I need to check Penny's mouth?"

"Peggy," she croaked.

"The ghost of your dead husband appears and your first instinct is to correct him." Greg's grin widened. "Honey, I'm home!"

Julie sagged against the wall, convinced she was having a nervous breakdown. Greg moved toward her and she noticed that he glided across the floor in a manner similar to the other hallucinations. Instinctively, she backed away.

Greg's mischievous smile faded. "Julie, talk to me," he urged.

Peggy jumped down from the windowsill and wandered over to investigate. The cat threaded her way through Greg's legs, avoiding his feet.

The cat was avoiding his feet.

"She can see you, too," Julie murmured. Maybe there was a reason Peggy had belonged to Inga. Or was Julie also imagining the cat's actions? Maybe this entire scene was a hallucination—or a dream. Maybe she'd wake up in bed and her mother would still be alive.

Julie squeezed her eyes shut. No, it wasn't a dream. She hosted her mother's memorial service. Her estranged brother was in town. She met with a lawyer.

"Jelly?"

Julie's stomach tightened at the sound of her secret nickname. Nobody knew about Peanut Butter and Jelly except she and her husband. On the night he proposed, he'd commented they went together like peanut butter and jelly and thus PB and Jelly were born.

Greg inched closer to her with his arms outstretched.

"No," Julie said, giving her head a violent shake. She promptly burst into tears and fled upstairs.

She face-planted on the bed and continued to cry. She knew she was rubbing snot all over her comforter, but she didn't care. There were more important concerns right now, like the fact that she was certifiably insane.

"Julie, I'm so sorry. I didn't mean to upset you."

Julie turned her head to look at him, leaving her cheek pressed against the comforter. "How did you think your presence would go over?"

He forced a smile. "I thought you'd be as happy to see me as I am to see you. How long has it been?"

As she studied his face, the fear began to subside. This was Greg, her husband. The love of her life.

"Two and a half years."

"Hmm. Feels like yesterday."

"And you're what—a ghost?"

"I don't see what else I can be." He gave her an appraising look. "Although I don't recall you possessing a sixth sense like that kid in the movie."

"I see dead people," she whispered, more to herself.

Greg reached for a tissue, but his hand went straight through the box. "Damn. I need to work on my poltergeist skills."

Julie pushed herself into a seated position and blinked away the tears that clung to her lashes. "It's really you."

He held out his arms. "It really is."

"Have you been here this whole time?" She grabbed a pillow and hugged it against her chest for comfort.

"You mean ever since I died? No, but I can't tell you where I've been." He shrugged. "No clue."

"What happened that would bring you here now?"

"Your mom died," he said pointedly. "Kind of a big deal."

"I know, but why would that summon your ghost and not hers?"

"I don't know. To comfort you?"

"Then why not comfort me after you died. That's when I really needed you." What could possibly have summoned him here now?

Julie slapped her forehead, feeling like a complete fool. The man in the suit, Rosie, and Bunny Slipper Babs weren't hallucinations. They were ghosts like Greg, triggered by her gift from Inga. Julie had finally inherited her magical asset.

"It was the cocktail," Julie said out loud.

Greg chuckled. "You're not drunk, Jelly. I promise this is not like that time in Mexico."

Julie laughed at the reference. She'd been so drunk on a vacation in Cozumel that she'd sworn she met a talking pig called Pedro and no one could persuade her otherwise.

"I don't mean a random cocktail." How could she explain that Inga's gift had manifested as a sixth sense? "Interesting things have happened since you died." She couldn't believe she hadn't put two and two together before now. In her defense, neither Libbie nor Kate had seen ghosts after drinking their cocktails, so it wasn't as though this particular skill was anticipated.

"I feel like I should be insulted," Greg said. "Are you suggesting your life was vanilla until I died and now it's awash in chocolate and sprinkles?"

"Jimmies," she corrected him, reigniting an old disagreement. "And I'm not suggesting anything of the kind. You should know that your wife is officially a witch."

"Well, I always knew that."

She tried to give him a playful punch, but her fist went straight through his arm. "Do you remember Inga Paulsen?"

"The cool old lady with all the husbands?"

"Three husbands," Julie clarified. "And she was even cooler than we realized." She proceeded to relay the events of the past seven months.

Greg whistled. "You realize how nuts that sounds, right? Hallucination actually seems like the more plausible explanation."

"Libbie and Kate haven't hallucinated. Trust me, we all saw Kate's wart. It was big enough for its own zip code."

Greg grinned. "Poor Kate. I can't imagine she handled that very well. She was always such a perfectionist."

His insight took Julie by surprise. "She was, but she's gotten a lot better with that. You should see her kids. And Libbie's. They're all so big now. Josh is even taller than my brother, if you can imagine that." She stopped talking abruptly at the mention of her brother.

"Does Brad know about your mom?"

She nodded, this morning's tension returning to her body. "He's freaking out that she left me the bulk of her estate."

Greg's eyes widened. "Wait. Brad is actually here in Lake Cloverleaf?"

Julie nodded. "Mom's lawyer tracked him down because she left him twenty grand."

Greg whistled. "That's nineteen thousand, nine hundred and ninety-nine dollars more than he deserved."

Julie smiled. She could always count on Greg to be on her side. Even when he didn't necessarily agree with her in family matters, he was always, unequivocally, on her side.

"He's furious that Mom left the house to me. He clearly planned to sell it and take half the profit."

Greg snorted. "This house? The one you and I took care of while we also took care of Doris when your brother couldn't be bothered?"

"That's the one."

"I'm sure I should be surprised, but that's such a typical Brad move." Greg seemed to notice the bedroom for the first time. "You haven't changed much in here."

"Why would I? We were both happy with the way it looked."

Greg pointed to the bedside table. "What's that?" He slid closer to inspect the box. "Why is my name inscribed on here?"

Her gaze flicked to the elegant marble box. "Because it's you."

Her husband's ghost balked. "Me?"

"Your ashes. I didn't want anyone to toss a pair of earrings in there for storage, hence the inscription."

Greg stared at the box in silence.

"What?"

He turned to look at her. "Why are you keeping me here by the bed?"

"Would you rather I display you on the mantel like a Christmas decoration?"

His expression softened. "Julie, this isn't good."

"Pipe down before I kick your ash." Julie waited for him to laugh at her dad joke, but he said nothing. "If you don't like the box, I can get another one. I wasn't exactly thinking clearly when I had to choose."

Greg shook his head. "That's not what I mean. I don't want you to have a box at all. You should spread my ashes somewhere scenic, not keep them next to your bed like a creepy companion. It's not healthy."

"You're not creepy," Julie said.

"No, but sleeping with my ashes is."

"I don't dress them up in cute boxers and lay them on the bed. *That* would be creepy."

Greg groaned. "Please don't keep them here. It weirds me out and I'm the one in there. How do you ever expect another man to spend the night with my ashes staring at him?"

Julie's eyes widened. "Why would another man spend the night?"

He maneuvered closer to her and rested his hands on her shoulders—sort of. "Julie Eloise Duncan. I have been dead and gone for two and a half years. Please tell me you've been on at least one date."

"I can tell you that, but it won't be true." She gazed into his eyes—those soulful brown eyes that comforted her in times of strife and made her feel like the sexiest woman in the world. Nobody looked at her the way Greg did. Not even Jared Kelley who was supposedly obsessed with her in tenth grade.

She reached for his cheek, but her hand slipped right through him. "I guess this means I can't kiss you either."

He shook his head sadly. "Afraid not. We're limited to eyeballing each other and having mesmerizing conservations, which still seems pretty amazing to me." He bent forward and brushed his lips against her forehead. Julie felt a flutter of air but nothing more.

It *was* amazing. Greg was here and she wasn't about to complain. That was Doris's territory.

"When you have some free time, do me a favor and scatter my ashes," he said.

"Where?"

Greg appeared thoughtful. "How about that overlook where we used to stop for a picnic when you insisted you couldn't manage another step without a Ho Ho?"

Julie hadn't hiked there in years. Once Greg became too sick to venture out in nature, Julie had stopped doing much of anything. No wonder she'd gained weight. It wasn't only menopause to blame. It was her own inertia.

"I'm not even sure if I could get up there without inducing an injury," she said.

"You can't be that out of shape," he said, angling his head. "Although your boobs do look bigger."

She glanced down at her chest. "Some of the extra pounds migrated there, so I guess it isn't all bad."

Greg splayed his hands in front of her boobs. "I wish I could I test them out."

"Test them?" she repeated, laughter bubbling in her throat. "They're not a chemistry experiment."

Greg gazed at her with such affection, she thought her heart would burst from pure joy. "God, I've missed you."

Her eyes moistened with a fresh batch of tears. "I've missed you, too." She inhaled sharply. "The cocktail club is meeting here tonight. What am I going to tell them?"

"If this whole magic thing is true, then I guess you tell them the truth. If anyone will understand, it's them."

"You're right." Still, the prospect made her anxious. What if they didn't believe her or thought she was out of her mind?

"I recognize that look in your eye," Greg said. "I saw it the day we got my diagnosis. Do you remember?"

"How could I forget?" It was one of the worst days of Julie's life, second only to his actual death.

He crooked a finger under her chin and it felt like a feather brushing against her skin. "Whatever this is, Julie, it's going to be okay."

"Of course it will," she said, her spirits lifting. Because Julie was no longer alone. Greg was back and they'd deal with this new normal the same way they'd dealt with every other curveball they'd been thrown—together.

SIX

By the time her friends arrived for cocktail club, Julie was in the midst of yet another hot flash triggered by stress. She tore off the extra layer and threw it on the back of the sofa.

"You look so angry when you do that," Greg said. "Like the Hulk, only much more attractive and with paler skin."

"Be grateful you're not around for menopause. It's a real bitch." Julie alternated between hot and cold so frequently that she found she had to dress in layers no matter what the weather. She never bothered with the buttons, knowing she'd be ripping off the layer multiple times a day.

"I'm not grateful. I'd choose more time with you no matter what phase of life you were in. Even if I showed up and you were pushing a walker around the house and searching for the glasses that were on a chain around your neck, I'd still want to be here."

Julie scrunched her nose. "You'd still look like this and I'd be a hag. No thanks."

The doorbell rang and Julie drew a quick breath.

"Showtime," Greg said.

Peggy zipped past them and bolted for the front door. The cat somehow knew her favorite people were on the doorstep.

The trio stood huddled together on the doorstep. Each woman carried a tote bag that appeared to be overflowing with bottles and boxes.

"Let us in. I'm freezing," Kate said, hopping up and down.

"That's because you don't have an ounce of fat on your body," Julie said. She stepped aside to let them pass.

"Wow. Tell them they haven't aged a day," Greg said. "Did Libbie always look this good?"

She shot him a menacing look but didn't respond. She ushered her friends into the kitchen where she'd prepared a few items for tasting.

"What's all this?" Libbie asked, her gaze sweeping the island. "We told you not to go to any trouble."

"Does this look like I went to any trouble?" Julie waved a hand in front of the display. She'd bought a selection of Pop-Tart flavors and paired them with different drinks. Her favorite frosted strawberry Pop-Tarts were paired with dry white wines. The chocolate flavor was paired with a pinot noir and the cinnamon flavor was paired with a Moscow mule.

"Holy empty calories I love this idea," Rebecca enthused.

Julie smiled. "Doris isn't here to condemn my choices, so I figured—why not?"

"I haven't had a Pop-Tart since I was a kid," Kate said, eyeing the selection. "I think I'll choose a flavor based on the drink I want."

"Whatever works for you," Julie said.

Libbie unpacked their tote bags and Julie spotted a plate of Libbie's famous homemade frosted brownies covered with plastic wrap.

"You're spoiling me," Julie said.

Kate took over bartending duties. "You deserve to be spoiled, Jules. You just lost your mom."

Julie didn't miss the pained look on her friend's face. She knew Kate was no stranger to losing a mother. Her own mother had committed suicide when Kate was a teenager.

Greg appeared in the kitchen and immediately spotted the brownies. "Oh, wow. I am so regretting my death right now."

Julie bit her lip to keep from responding.

"Let's start with our compliment circle," Libbie suggested. "I suspect Julie could use a few positive remarks right now."

Greg arched an eyebrow. "What's a compliment circle? You never mentioned that. I thought you just drank and complained about the menfolk in your lives."

"Sounds good to me," Rebecca said. She plucked a glass of pinot noir off the counter.

Kate nodded. "I'll mix more cocktails for the second round, unless you want to stick with Pop-Tart pairings."

Julie poured a glass of sauvignon blanc and joined her friends in the family room. Libbie sat in the cushioned chair and Julie perched on the ottoman in front of her.

Greg wore a goofy grin as he settled himself between Kate and Rebecca on the sofa like he was one of the girls. "I can't wait to hear this."

Julie shushed him, prompting a look of surprise from the other women.

"We haven't even started yet," Kate said.

"If you don't feel up to receiving compliments, just tell us," Rebecca added. "We won't force you."

"Tell them you feel up to it," Greg said. "I need to be a fly on the wall for this conversation."

"I'm fine with it," Julie said. "It's been quite a day, to be honest. I'll tell you all about it after my second drink."

"That bad, huh?" Rebecca asked.

"It's pretty unbelievable," Julie said cryptically.

"Whatever it is, we know you can handle it because you're a superstar," Libbie said.

Kate shot her a quizzical look. "Is that your compliment?"

Libbie shifted awkwardly in the chair. "You don't think that counts?"

"Come on. You can do better," Kate urged.

"You seem like you're phoning it in," Rebecca agreed.

Greg clapped his hands. "This is great. Are they always this entertaining?"

Libbie drew a deep breath and tried again. "Julie, if Courtney is half the daughter to me that you were to Doris, I'll be one of the luckiest moms in the world." She gave the other two women a pointed look. "Satisfied?"

"Better." Kate lifted her chin a fraction. "Julie, your authenticity continues to inspire me each and every day."

Greg flashed a smile and gave Julie a thumbs up.

"You make me want to be a better person," Rebecca said.

"Hey, that's cheating," Libbie said. "It's from *As Good As It Gets*."

"She's right, it is," Greg said.

"Technically, Jack Nicholson says she makes him want to be a better man," Kate replied.

Rebecca frowned. "So what? One guy says it in a movie and now it's off limits to everyone else?"

"It's okay," Julie said. "I accept the compliment."

"Good because it's true." Rebecca folded her arms and glowered at Kate. "You say you feel the need for speed on your boat all the time and nobody ever tells you that belongs to Tom Cruise."

Kate glowered. "Fine, I will no longer say I feel the need for speed. Happy now?"

"Ladies," Libbie said, stretching out the word. "This is a difficult time for Julie and I think we're making it worse."

"Not for me," Greg interjected. "This is totally worth the price of admission."

"Who's ready for a second round?" Julie asked. She was ready to share, but she needed a bit more liquid courage first.

"We haven't finished our compliment circle," Kate argued.

"This is Julie's evening," Libbie said. "If she wants to move on to the second round, that's what we do."

"Then I'd better get started on those cocktails." Kate rose to her feet and strode into the kitchen.

Julie focused on the sound of the ice crashing together in the shaker as she gathered her wits. She wasn't entirely sure where to start. By the time Kate handed her a sweaty glass filled to the brim with a brandy Old-Fashioned, Julie's stomach was in such knots, she was ready to spill her actual guts.

"How was the meeting with the lawyer?" Rebecca asked.

Kate's face registered surprise. "You haven't told her yet?"

Julie downed the drink and slammed the empty glass on the coffee table. "I see dead people," she blurted.

"Nice," Greg said, his head bobbing. "Very casual."

Libbie glanced from Kate to Rebecca. "Did she just tell us she sees dead people?"

"I think so." Kate sipped her cocktail. "Jules, honey. Did you tell us you can see ghosts?"

Wordlessly, Julie nodded.

"She needs another drink," Greg said, pointing to the empty glass.

"Kate, would you mind mixing her another drink?" Rebecca asked.

Greg motioned to Rebecca. "I knew I liked you."

Kate seemed reluctant to return to the kitchen in case she missed anything. She kept her gaze pinned on Julie.

"The night of my mom's memorial service, a cocktail recipe appeared in my book and I drank it," Julie said.

The three women gasped.

"And you're only telling us now?" Kate asked.

"Honestly, it slipped my mind," Julie said. "The next morning I saw a man in the grocery store and I thought I was hallucinating. It didn't occur to me that he might be a ghost." She told them about Barbara and Rosie, too.

"When did you realize they were ghosts?" Libbie asked.

Julie's gaze darted to Greg. "When my husband showed up."

"What?" Rebecca screeched.

Greg's hands flew to cover his ears. "Good thing we don't have a dog."

"You've actually seen Greg?" Kate hurried back to the family room with a tray of fresh cocktails and quickly distributed them.

"He's right there." Julie gestured to his place on the sofa.

Rebecca reeled back. "Right here?"

"He's been sitting between you and Kate."

Greg slapped his hands on his thighs. "Tell them they all look amazing, but don't add 'for their age.' Nobody likes that."

Julie cleared her throat. "He says you all look great."

Rebecca scooched to the end of the sofa. "Does he look like... himself?"

"Who else would I look like?" Greg rubbed his chin thoughtfully. "I wonder if I can change my appearance the way I can change my clothes."

"Please don't change your appearance," Julie said. She liked her husband just as he was. "Other than being slightly transparent, he looks normal," she told the others.

The three women stared at the empty cushion on the sofa.

"This is amazing," Libbie said. "What a gift."

Greg flexed his arms before placing his hands behind his head. "I really am."

"What happened with the other ghosts you saw?" Kate asked.

Julie shrugged. "Nothing. I didn't realize what was happening at the time. Now I know."

"What will you do if you see another one?" Rebecca shuddered. "I'm glad this is your inheritance and not mine. I'd be too freaked out."

"Speaking of freaked out, tell them about Brad," Greg prompted.

"I already told Kate, but my brother is in town," Julie said.

"Wow. And the hits just keep coming," Rebecca breathed.

Julie told them about the meeting with the lawyer.

"I'm glad she left you everything," Libbie said. "You deserve it."

"I'm worried about Brad," Julie admitted. "He was so angry."

"Brad can take a short walk off a long pier," Kate said.

Rebecca laughed. "I think you mean that the other way around."

"Good thing I'm the designated driver tonight," Libbie said.

Julie grabbed a blanket from the back of the cushioned chair and wrapped it around her shoulders. "Honestly, I'm more concerned about the dead than the living. What if ghosts start popping up everywhere I go? I nearly lost my mind in the middle of the grocery store."

"You know the question to ask," Libbie said.

"Valium or Xanax?" Kate quipped.

"How can you make this experience the best thing that ever happened to you?" Libbie asked. "That's what you said to me when I first freaked out over my gift, remember?"

Julie remembered. "But this is different."

Libbie cocked an eyebrow. "How?"

"Because it's happening to me."

The other women laughed.

"If you can see ghosts, maybe we should summon Inga," Kate said.

"Great idea," Rebecca replied. "It would be amazing to have her with us again, even if Julie was the only one who could communicate with her."

Greg blinked. "Am I not a good enough ghost?"

Libbie turned to look at Kate. "Do you think that's even possible?"

Kate shrugged. "Why not? Stranger things have happened, especially to us."

"We tried before and it didn't work," Julie said.

"We tried with a pot-smoking witch," Kate said. "We should try something else."

Julie shook her head. "No. Don't you remember what Lorraine said? Witches don't hang around. I'm paraphrasing, but it was something like their spirits have better places to be."

Libbie nodded. "Julie's right."

"Anyway, as nice as it would be to see Inga again, I think one ghost in my house is more than enough."

Greg held up his hand for a high-five, but Julie ignored him.

Kate shook the ice in her glass. "In that case, how can you make this experience with your husband's ghost the best thing that's ever happened to you?"

Libbie wore a dreamy smile. "Now I'm picturing Patrick Swayze, Demi Moore, and a clay pot."

Greg winked at his wife. "I like where this is headed."

Julie's cheeks burned at the thought of erotic clay making with her dead husband. "I appreciate the support, but I think I'm going to take this one day at a time."

Kate nodded her approval. "Smart."

"If there's something's strange in your neighborhood..." Rebecca began.

Julie held up a silencing hand. "No Ghostbusters. Seriously. Just don't."

Kate snapped her fingers. "What was that creepy movie with Nicole Kidman where she and the kids think they see ghosts, but it turns out they *are* the ghosts?"

Libbie hopped up and down on the chair. "Ooh. *The Others!*"

"Spoiler alert," Rebecca grumbled.

"What are you suggesting?" Julie asked, frowning. "That we're all ghosts?"

"No," Kate said. "We were naming ghost movies."

"We really weren't," Greg interjected.

"If I were a ghost, I'd be a lot more flexible," Julie said. "And I wouldn't have cramps or insomnia or night sweats."

"Or painful joints," Rebecca added.

"Or vaginal dryness," Libbie chimed in.

Greg grimaced. "Okay, I'm starting to regret my presence here."

Julie couldn't help but laugh at her husband's discomfort. Served him right for eavesdropping.

Kate raised her glass. "Cheers to Julie, our very own ghost whisperer."

Julie lifted her glass to join the others. She was a ghost whisperer. The Greg part was amazing; it was dealing with other ghosts that made her wary. As excited as she wanted to be over finally receiving her gift, Julie couldn't help but feel that she wanted to return it.

SEVEN

Julie spent the next morning nursing a hangover. She opened one eye to see Greg watching her with an amused expression.

"Were you watching me sleep?" Julie asked, pulling herself to a seated position.

"No, I was watching you toss and turn," he said. "Were you always this active at night? It was like watching a tennis match and you were the ball."

"I'm uncomfortable and I never sleep through the night anymore," she said.

He gave her a sympathetic look. "Men really have no idea what women go through."

"Thank you," she said.

"You'd better hurry up and get dressed. Someone's about to..."

Julie heard the sound of the front door open. She cast a curious look at Greg. "Who's that?"

"Jules, are you decent?" Brad's voice rang out.

Julie's eyes widened. "What's he doing here?"

"I don't know, but he's not alone."

Julie broke into a cold sweat and leaped out of bed to change into sweatpants and a T-shirt. She pulled her hair into a loose ponytail and hurried downstairs.

She found Brad in the formal dining room with a woman in a white blouse and dress pants. Her red hair was perfectly coiffed, as though she'd come straight from the salon.

"Who's this?" Julie asked, eyeing the woman with trepidation.

"Hi, I'm MaryAnn Bigglesworth," she said.

Brad stepped forward. "MaryAnn is a realtor and she's going to recommend a sale price for the house."

Julie frowned. "Why would she do that?"

"That's usually a requirement when you sell a house," Brad said.

Julie folded her arms and fixed him with a hard look. "What makes you think I'm selling the house?"

"If you're going to buy me out, I guess that works, too, but I figure you don't have that kind of money."

Anger coiled in Julie's stomach. "Brad, you attended the same meeting I did. You know this house doesn't belong to you in any way, shape, or form."

MaryAnn's gaze darted from brother to sister. "You know what? I'd be happy to come back another time, once you've had a chance to iron out the details."

Brad kept his eyes pinned on Julie. "There's nothing to iron out. We're going to sell the house and split the proceeds in half."

Julie licked her lips, unsure how to proceed. She didn't want to set off Brad's temper or embarrass the realtor.

"You can't sell what you don't own," Julie said.

"That's very true," MaryAnn said. She adjusted her purse strap. "Give me a call if and when you're ready to proceed." She smiled. "For what it's worth, it's a spectacular property. If you want to sell, I think it would make a fabulous bed and breakfast. There's no place in town with a comparable view." Her heels clicked across the wooden floor as she made her way out of the house.

Brad glowered at Julie. "What in the hell did you do that for?"

"I don't know what you think you're doing, but the lawyer told you very clearly that Mom left the house to me." She spoke quietly, wary of igniting his temper. She'd witnessed enough of his teenaged tantrums to know she didn't want to be on the receiving end of one.

"Then I suggest we schedule another meeting with the lawyer so we can fix that problem."

Julie thought she'd been experiencing an alternate reality with the ghosts, but Brad was taking things to a whole new level.

"I'm glad he left town when he did," Greg said. "Imagine if you had to put up with this nonsense every day."

Julie couldn't imagine. Her mother had been challenging enough.

"Call the lawyer now," Brad demanded. "I'll wait." He strode into the kitchen and seated himself at the table by the window. It was one of Julie's favorite spots in the house and she resented his presence there. He was going to taint it with his negative energy.

"Brad, I don't think you understand how wills work. We can't tell the lawyer to change it."

"Maybe not, but you can have him draw up paperwork to give half of your inheritance to me." His lips curved into a malevolent smile. "Don't worry, you don't have to be dead to transfer half your assets."

Julie gaped at him in disbelief. "Why would I do that?"

"Because I told you to and you, little sister, always do as you're told." He leaned back against the chair and stretched his legs. "Where's your phone?"

"Tell him to shove the phone up his ass," Greg said, materializing next to Julie. "Don't you dare call the lawyer. He's not getting a single penny from you."

Julie didn't know what to do. She didn't want to call the lawyer, but equally, she didn't want to draw her brother's ire. Her hands trembling, Julie pulled her phone from her pocket and searched for the lawyer's information. She wished her mother had used Libbie's boyfriend to handle the estate instead. Julie trusted Ethan Townsend and knew he'd have a way of handling Brad that protected Julie.

"You need to tell him no," Greg insisted.

Julie would talk to Greg afterward. Right now, she'd placate Brad if only so he would leave the house.

"It's Saturday, Brad. No one's going to be in the office, but I'll call on Monday."

Brad regarded her coolly. "Call now and leave a voicemail. That way they'll call you back first thing in the morning on Monday."

Julie swallowed hard and dialed. At the prompt, she pressed three and waited to be transferred to Howard's voicemail.

"Hi. This is Julie Duncan, Doris's daughter. I'd like to make another appointment with Howard. If someone could call me on Monday morning, I'd really appreciate it. I want to talk to him about the inheritance and discuss a couple of options with him. Thanks so much." She left her number and set the phone on the counter. "I'll let you know as soon as he calls back."

Brad tipped an imaginary hat. "Good job, sis. I guess this means I'm staying in town a little longer. Gives us time to catch up." He winked at her. "See you later."

"Good riddance, jackass," Greg said.

Julie watched her brother exit the kitchen, silently cursing him with every step. She wanted so much to like her brother—love him even—but Brad's behavior made it impossible for her to feel anything except contempt.

Libbie cooked to work through her frustrations. Kate exercised. Rebecca cuddled an animal.

Julie cleaned.

Following her brother's unexpected and unpleasant visit, she marched straight upstairs and tackled her mother's bathroom. It was good timing. She'd already cleared the room of her mother's toiletries and removed all the towels for washing. All that was left was a deep scrub.

"Any chance you could do this in a thong and nothing else?" Greg asked.

Julie was on her knees scrubbing the bottom of the bathtub. She twisted to give him an incredulous look. "You really have been dead for two and a half years if you think this booty still looks good in a thong."

"I wish you would take your aggression out on your brother instead of the bathtub," he said.

Julie huffed and turned back to the tub. "You don't understand. He's my brother."

"That's the same excuse you gave every time I suggested taking a tougher stance with your mother."

She flipped onto her bottom and leaned her back against the side of the tub. "You know I hate confrontation."

"Because you've spent your whole life being dominated by other people in your family. Let your mother's death be the end of it."

Julie toyed with the sponge, thinking. "I'll talk to Howard and see if he can help me deal with Brad."

"Howard isn't on your side," Greg reminded her. "He was your mother's lawyer and he represents her estate, not you."

"Exactly, and if we can get Howard to say he isn't taking new clients, then Brad will have to wait until we find someone else."

Greg floated over to hover over the edge of the sink. "It's a decent stalling tactic, but it doesn't solve the problem. He's just going to find another lawyer willing to work with you. The only way to handle it is to tell him no. He's a bully."

"I'm used to bullies," Julie said with a sigh of resignation. As she shifted back to her knees to finish cleaning the tub, she felt a drop of liquid on her shoulder. "What on earth?" She touched the material of her top where a small wet circle had appeared. Instinctively, Julie glanced up at the ceiling. A wet spot about the size of a cereal bowl had formed on the plaster. Not ideal.

Greg followed her gaze. "Want me to check it out? I don't even need a ladder. One of the perks of being incorporeal." His form dissipated and he returned a moment later, his expression grim.

"Bad news. You're going to need to call a roofer. Did you have a storm recently?"

"The other night," Julie said. "I heard it when I was lying awake in bed."

"Well, it caused some damage. I wouldn't put it off."

Ugh. This was not what Julie wanted to hear. It was a weekend, which meant she'd probably get charged an exorbitant fee for an emergency visit. If only she could fix it herself. Greg had been the handy one, though. Julie wasn't incompetent, but she wasn't great with ladders and her fine motor skills seemed to be deteriorating along with her eyesight. There was a point in time when Julie pictured herself like Monica Bellucci, able to play the role of Bond Girl at fifty. Instead, she seemed to be turning into Sophia Petrillo from *The Golden Girls*. Like Libbie once said, straight from a nursing bra to a nursing home, not that Julie had ever owned a nursing bra. She was grateful to still have relatively perky boobs for her age.

"Do you think I could fix it myself if you talked me through it?" Julie asked.

Greg shook his head. "It would've been above my pay grade even when I was solid."

She tossed the sponge over her shoulder and into the tub. "Maybe Brad's right. Maybe I should sell." After all, the house was much too big for one person.

"Don't do that," Greg said.

She looked up at him. "Do what?"

"You're letting one problem stop you from getting what you want. It's a roof. You call someone and they fix it."

"And that someone costs money. And then there will be another expensive problem after that. Meanwhile, I'll have Brad breathing down my neck." She buried her face in her hands. "I can't do this."

Greg lowered himself to the floor to be next to her. "One step at a time, Julie. You're more powerful than you realize. You got through cancer with me. You got through your mom. You'll get through this, too."

Julie slid her hands back to her sides. "Thanks for the pep talk. I'm just feeling overwhelmed and this leak isn't helping."

"Find a roofer," Greg said. "That's step one. Ernie Peterman retired or I'd say to call him. I'm sure one of your friends can recommend somebody."

She gulped down the lump in her throat and nodded. "You're right. I'll do it now."

Greg smiled. "That's my girl. I'm going to disappear for a bit, if that's okay."

Julie flinched. "Disappear? What do you mean?"

"There are a few people I'd like to check on," he said. "I've been so happy to see you again, that it didn't occur to me to visit anyone else."

"They won't be able to see you," Julie reminded him.

"I know, but I'd still like to check in with Pete and Jamie. See if they still suck at racquetball."

"Of course. Go. I need to call the roofers anyway and that's about as boring as it gets." Julie climbed to her feet, her legs sore from the way she'd been seated.

Greg planted an airy kiss on her forehead. "Love you. I'll be back in a bit."

"Love you, too."

Once he'd disappeared, Julie sent a group text requesting recommendations. Knowing Kate, she had an Excel spreadsheet of tradespeople with star ratings as well as a summary of their pros and cons. Sure enough, she received two immediate replies with names. She called both to get more than one estimate.

After scheduling the appointments, Julie carried her laptop downstairs to the kitchen table. In light of the repairs that would inevitably be needed and her inheritance, now seemed like a reasonable time to engage in a financial State of the Union.

With its large and airy rooms, high property taxes, and prominent lakeside position, the house was expensive to maintain. Her father's pension had passed to Doris upon his death, but those payments ceased now that Doris was gone. Last year when the heating system had to be replaced, Julie used the remainder of her savings to pay for it. In terms of cash, she was down to her mother's savings and a modest life insurance payout, minus the twenty thousand that would go to Brad. The situation wasn't dire, except Julie knew all too well that the unexpected could happen. The air conditioner could break. Her car could need a new engine. Julie could end up in the hospital with bills that insurance refused to cover. The list was endless.

She fully intended to work now that she no longer had to provide full-time care for her mother. It was simply a matter of figuring out what she wanted to do and whether it would pay enough to sustain her. She was only fifty. She couldn't afford to coast on financial fumes until her demise.

Her mind flitted back to the visit from Brad's realtor. Again, she considered whether it made financial sense to sell. She wouldn't give Brad half the proceeds, of course. She could use the money to buy a smaller, more manageable house in cash and not worry about mortgage payments.

Except Julie didn't want to sell.

Her gaze drifted to the family room where she'd accumulated so many memories. She'd spent the majority of her life in this house. Despite her difficult relationship with her mother, Julie wasn't without fond memories of her. Doris had been a willing shopper and always made sure to buy Julie the most wanted toy at the top of her Christmas list. After a snowfall, they'd huddle near the fireplace and drink hot chocolate as they admired the winter wonderland outside.

She and Greg spent many happy evenings curled up on the sofa together, watching *Star Wars* or enjoying a glass of wine together after a long day. He'd even proposed in that very room, after seeking her mother's permission, of course. Doris had later commented to friends that his request was the mark of a good man. Julie's chest had puffed with pride when she overheard the remark.

What had the realtor said? *If you want to sell, I think it would make a fabulous bed and breakfast.* The idea had merit, except Julie wanted to keep the house, not sell it. Converting the house into a bed and breakfast could be the answer to her problem. If she earned enough from the endeavor, she could afford the maintenance long-term, as well as replenish her savings. But how much would it cost to convert the house to a bed and breakfast and could she handle the workload?

"You look smart right now."

Julie peered over the top of the computer to smile at Greg. "It's my reading glasses, isn't it?"

"Put your hair up in a bun and you'll give off that sexy librarian vibe."

Julie removed the glasses and set them on the table. "I guess I got these after you died. See? Everything went downhill from there, including my vision."

"You would've needed reading glasses regardless of whether I lived or died," Greg said. "It's one of those aging things."

Julie looked him squarely in the face. "Be honest. Do I look older to you?"

Greg recoiled. "I sense this is one of those no-win situations."

"When you first saw me again, did you notice anything different, aside from bigger boobs?"

Greg pretended to zip his lip. "Again, I see no good answer to that question."

"You're already dead. What's the worst I can do to you?"

"You can be upset with me," Greg said, completely serious. "I don't know how long I'm here and I don't want to spend a minute of it with you being upset."

A lump formed in Julie's throat at the prospect of losing Greg all over again. "We have no reason to believe you'll be snapped back to the void, or wherever you came from."

Greg gave her a long look. "Jelly, it's naive to think I'll be here forever. At some point, whatever brought me here is going to take me back. It's inevitable."

"Stop saying that." Julie's jaw tensed. "How were Pete and Jamie?"

"They seem fine. They were both in the middle of household projects. Pete was fixing a sink and Jamie was pumping up his son's bike tire."

"Sounds like a typical day in suburbia."

She turned her attention back to the screen and Greg drifted over to her side of the computer. "Are you watching porn again?" he asked.

Julie tried to give him a playful smack, but her hand went right through him. "This is not porn. It's my finances. I'm trying to figure out next steps."

"I hope your next step doesn't involve Brad."

"Not if I can help it."

"You can help it, Julie. He can't force you to give him anything. His only option is to contest the will, but I would think any decent lawyer would tell him it's a waste of time and money." Greg reviewed the numbers on the spreadsheet. "Hmm. I didn't exactly leave you a windfall, did I?"

"It wasn't your fault."

"Cancer is expensive when your insurance sucks."

"Cancer cost you your life. It's expensive in every sense of the word." Julie didn't want him to feel responsible. It wasn't as though Greg burned through money because he liked to make frivolous purchases. The fight against cancer depleted their spirits as well as their savings.

"Maybe if I'd taken a job with better insurance, you'd have more in the bank now. Rick always bragged about how great his healthcare was with UPS. I should've paid closer attention."

Julie didn't want Greg to have regrets. She would be fine financially. She could always make more money, but she couldn't make another Greg.

"I'm focused on the future, not the past," Julie said.

Greg smirked. "That's not entirely true."

"You're not the past. You're my present."

"I certainly am. A gift in every sense of the word." He leaned over and brushed his lips against hers. Julie felt a slight tickle.

"I'm mulling over the idea of turning this house into a bed and breakfast," Julie said. "I think it has a lot of benefits."

"Such as?"

"It's a way of earning money and keeping the house. I'd meet interesting people. Show off our fabulous lake view."

"You never did like an office environment, did you?" Greg mused.

"No, it didn't suit me. The second anyone invited me to a conference room to celebrate a random colleague's birthday, I'd want to run for cover."

"But you're missing out on the free cake."

"I'll serve my own cake here and no one will have to sing for it."

Greg appeared to consider the idea. "This is a huge house for one person."

"And we don't have kids to leave it to when I'm gone," Julie added.

"Any regrets about that, now that I'm gone?"

She'd asked herself the same question after he died. She and Greg were childless by choice. Of course, they made that decision when they were younger and healthier and assumed they'd spend another fifty years together. Unfortunately, the universe had other plans.

"I thought about it," she admitted, "but the answer would still be no."

Greg's relief was palpable. "For what it's worth, I think the B&B is a stellar idea. You should go for it."

Julie brightened. "Really? You're not just humoring me?"

"I might make you laugh, Julie Duncan, but I never humor you."

Julie's smile widened to the point where she could feel the strain on her cheeks. "This is exciting. I have so much research to do now."

"That's always been one of your strengths," Greg said.

Julie knew what he was thinking. When he was first diagnosed, Julie spent countless hours researching treatments, both traditional and alternative. She read medical journals and basically anything she could access that related to pancreatic cancer. It was all for nothing, though. Cancer was determined to take him and all the research in the world couldn't save him.

"I'll start with the cost to see if it's even feasible. There's no point calling the zoning board or whoever else needs to get involved if I know I can't afford the basics." She figured each bedroom would need its own bathroom, which they currently didn't have. That would be a significant expense.

"I'm happy to do whatever I can to help," Greg offered. "If you want to leave a bunch of articles open on the computer, I can read them."

"If only you could touch things," Julie said.

He wiggled his eyebrow. "If only, indeed."

"Can you touch anything? I thought ghosts could throw things around a room and make a general nuisance of themselves."

"It's not like they offered a tutorial before I came back," he said.

She leaned her elbow on the table. "I guess that's another thing we can research while we're at it."

Greg pretended to roll up his sleeves. "You're in charge now."

Julie straightened in the chair, feeling emboldened. For the first time in her life, she was.

EIGHT

Julie awoke the next morning feeling better than she had in years. Her decision to start a bed and breakfast made her feel lighter somehow, as though an invisible weight had been lifted.

There was no sign of Greg, so she meandered downstairs to make a cup of tea and continue her research from the day before. She sat at the kitchen table and took a moment to admire the sunrise that illuminated the lake. The sky was awash in pale pink and burnt sienna. Winter was the season with the most dramatic sunrises and Julie figured it was nature's way of apologizing for the slush and ice.

Sipping a cup of mint tea, she finished reading yet another online article about starting a bed and breakfast. She wasn't sure how many she'd feel the need to read before she actually decided to commit. The information was roughly the same in each piece. The importance of location. The low profit margin. The taxes to consider. The zoning. She finally recognized that she was stalling because she was afraid to make a wrong choice.

"How am I fifty years old and still afraid of messing up?" she asked Peggy, who was luxuriating on the sunlit windowsill. "Shouldn't I have it all figured out by now?"

She knew better, really. Even Kate, her most together friend, had suffered a mini crisis recently where her life seemed to be falling apart before her eyes. Kate had to learn to let go and not worry so much about perfection. It had been a hard but worthwhile lesson.

"You look very intense right now." Greg glided into the kitchen, looking almost transparent in the bright sunlight.

"Where do you go when you're not here?"

"Depends. Today I went to the bakery."

Julie lifted her brow. "No, you did not."

He grinned and hooked his thumbs through the loopholes of his jeans. "Sure did."

Greg had suggested many times over the years that the owner of a local bakery was having an affair with the neighboring owner of a dry-cleaning business.

"And?" Julie prompted. Now that he'd gone to the trouble of playing ghost detective, she wanted to know the outcome.

"Relationship status confirmed," he said, and pumped a fist in the air. "I saw them canoodling in the back room."

Julie exhaled dreamily. "Ah, love among the glazed donuts."

"You owe me twenty bucks."

She gave him a wry look. "I'm sure that money will come in handy for you now." She leaned back against the slats of the wooden chair. "Can you think of any nice inns here? The Gaslamp is a motel, so it's not comparable." It was also located on the outskirts of town and catered to truckers and other people simply passing through. Julie wanted to attract a different clientele.

"There aren't that many houses left like this one," he said. "Most of them have been turned into professional offices."

She nodded. "The only places I can think of are The Dragonfly Inn and The White House and neither one has a view as pretty as ours."

Greg turned to admire the shimmering lake and smiled. "It is stunning, isn't it? We were lucky to live here."

The sound of the door startled her and she jumped to her feet. Her mouth dropped open when Brad swaggered into the kitchen.

Peggy jumped down to intercept him and he used his foot to nudge her out of the way, setting Julie's teeth on edge.

"Hey, sis. Got anything to eat? I'm starving and the motel doesn't serve breakfast."

"It's Sunday morning," Julie said. "What are you doing here so early?" Or at all.

"I thought we might enjoy a nice omelet and discuss our situation. If we can hammer out the details before we meet with the lawyer, we can both save ourselves some money. No point in lining the pockets of fat cats."

Inwardly, Julie groaned.

"Tell him he can't keep coming in here unannounced," Greg urged. "This isn't his house."

Julie felt torn. She didn't want to aggravate her brother and suffer the consequences. He was like their mother in that way, except bigger and stronger.

"If you keep letting him act without consequences, he'll never stop," her husband said.

Greg was right. Brad was a bully and, even if she managed to delay a meeting with the lawyer, he wasn't going to stop pushing her.

Julie mustered enough courage to speak. "You can't just keep waltzing in like you own the place—because you don't." Her voice sounded weak to her ears and she silently berated herself.

Brad's mouth twisted into an amused smile. "Seems like someone's lit a fire in your belly. What happened? You talk to that uppity friend of yours? What's her name—Kate?"

Julie's hands shook as they cemented to her hips. "You need to knock or ring the bell like everybody else or you won't be welcome here anymore."

Brad towered over her. He was a good five inches taller than she was, which made him seem even more intimidating.

"I said I'm hungry. Why don't you cook me breakfast and we'll see if we can't reach some kind of arrangement?"

Julie didn't know what kind of arrangement he had in mind,

but she felt compelled to hear him out. Maybe then he'd go away and stop pestering her.

She opened the refrigerator and pulled out a pint of soy milk. "There's cereal in the pantry."

"I can't believe you're feeding this slimeball," Greg complained.

At least she wasn't cooking for him. All he had to do was pour milk and cereal in the bowl.

Brad emerged from the pantry with a box of Cheerios. "I should've known you weren't capable of cooking. No wonder Mom died. She probably hadn't been fed properly for years."

Julie's whole body tensed.

"Now I really wish I could touch something," Greg said, planting a fist in the palm of his other hand.

Julie watched as her brother splattered milk all over the counter. He carried his bowl of cereal to the table and sat in her chair. She hurried to move the laptop before he spilled milk on that, too.

"What? You're afraid I'll see all your secrets? Don't worry, Jules. I read your diary in high school and there wasn't anything interesting in there. I doubt your life's gotten better."

Julie bristled with anger. Brad had always been off-putting, but she didn't remember him being as bad as this. She'd probably blocked it out.

"This milk is sour," he complained, but continued to eat.

"It's soy."

"Gross." He dragged the back of his hand across his mouth. "Got any beer left?"

Julie couldn't disguise her surprise. "Are you serious?"

"It's for later. I've got one of those little fridges in my room at the motel. I'll take it with me."

Julie rose to her feet and dutifully retrieved the beer. She wanted to scream, but it served no purpose. There was nothing she could do. It was the same when her mother would demand compliance. There was no point in arguing or refusing. It would only escalate the situation and Julie hated a scene. Better to acquiesce.

"I was looking up property values last night and I think we can net a pretty penny for this place." Milk and cereal spilled from the spoon as he brought it to his mouth.

Greg gave Julie a pointed look. "Tell him."

"Brad, I'm not giving you half of the house," Julie said. She brought her mug to her mouth. The tea was cold by now, but she didn't care. She only wanted something to hide behind.

Despite his apparent disgust, Brad drank the remaining milk straight from the bowl. Slowly, he set down the bowl and leveled her with a look. "Then you can buy me out."

"No. I won't do that either." She gripped the mug with both hands. It was substantial enough to wield as a weapon if necessary, although she couldn't picture herself in a physical altercation with her brother. They'd only ever exchanged sharp words, not sharp knives.

His expression hardened. "This is our family home..."

"Yes, you said that, but the fact remains that Mom left it to me and I put a lot of my own money into this house over the years, not to mention I gave up my job to take care of her." Julie's stomach squeezed as she waited for her brother's response.

"Good job," Greg said, giving her a thumbs up. Ghost or not, Julie felt better about speaking up with him in the room.

"What are your plans for the house then? The taxes are expensive, you know. It's an old house. Things will need to be repaired and replaced pretty often."

"I'm well aware of the cost associated with this house, thank you." It was incredibly rich of Brad to act like the foremost authority on a house she'd taken care of for years. At least he didn't know about the roof or he'd throw that in her face as though it was somehow her fault.

"How do you intend to afford the upkeep? You said yourself you gave up your job for Mom. It's not like you're qualified to do much and you're too old to start over now."

Greg swung a fist at Brad's head and it cut straight through. The top of her brother's hair shifted slightly in response to the movement.

"There's a draft in here," Brad said, smoothing his wayward strands of hair. "You might want to get that looked at by a professional. Could be a sign of a bigger problem."

The only sign of a bigger problem was sitting at her kitchen table.

"What's your goal here, Brad?" Julie asked. "Do you think if you scare me enough with the cost that I'll change my mind and hand over the house?"

"Or let me invest my twenty thousand so that we can fix it up for a bigger profit when we sell it."

He was still stuck on selling it and pocketing half the money. "Are you desperate for money or something? Don't you have a job in Phoenix, or wherever it is you live now?"

"I got laid off three months ago. Another stupid merger." The muscle in Brad's cheek pulsed. He tapped the spoon noisily on the edge of the bowl.

"The thing is, Brad, I've decided to turn the house into a bed and breakfast."

Brad's mocking laughter rang in her ears. "You're going to run a B&B? I don't think so."

She stiffened. "What's wrong with that? The house is too big for me and it's got a premium view with lake access."

There were four bedrooms that could be converted to guest rooms, allowing Julie to keep her current bedroom. She didn't want to leave the space that she'd once shared with Greg. She liked to linger in that hazy sliver of time between dreams and reality where Greg was still alive.

"I don't want strangers staying here. It's weird."

"It isn't up to you," Julie said.

"The hell it isn't. I grew up in this house, too. I get a say in what happens to it."

Julie licked her lips, trying to remain calm. "No, you don't. I'm in charge now. Mom left it to me."

"Only because you made her feel guilty."

Julie's mouth dropped open. "*I* made *her* feel guilty? You can't be serious."

"What's it called—undue influence?" Brad tossed the spoon into the bowl with a clatter.

"I'm not some random nurse who appeared on the scene in her final hours. I'm her daughter and I took care of her for years. Where were you, Brad? You couldn't even be bothered to visit once a year."

He pointed an angry finger at her. "I'm not letting you turn our family home into a business and that's the end of it."

They stared at each other for a tense moment.

"I think you should leave now," Julie said.

"You don't give me orders." He folded his arms across his chest. "I'll go when I damn well please."

An apple flew across the room and hit the side of Brad's head. "What the hell?" Brad gaped at her.

"That wasn't me," Julie said.

"The hell it wasn't. There's no one else here." He glared at her as he rubbed the side of his head.

"Do I look like Elastigirl to you?" She extended her arms and wiggled her fingers. "I can't reach the fruit bowl from here."

Brad shoved back his chair and stood. "This isn't the end of it, Julie. I don't care how many apples you throw at me." He stalked out of the kitchen and Julie waited until she heard the door slam shut to run and lock the door behind him.

"Did you see that?" Greg asked. "I moved something!"

She couldn't resist a smile. "Hard to miss it."

He rubbed his earlobe. "Yeah, sorry about that. I lost my temper." He paused and looked at her. "I wish you would've lost yours."

Julie sighed. "And what? Get into a fistfight with my stronger brother? I'm an out-of-shape fifty-year-old woman. I'd end up in the ER."

"You have to stand up to bullies or they'll keep up their bad behavior. Didn't your mother ever teach you that?" He stopped talking and closed his eyes. "No, of course not. Your mother *was* the bully."

Julie didn't want to continue the conversation. She was worn out from Brad's visit and it was only morning. "I feel like I made my point."

"You did well, Jelly. I'm proud of you, but Brad is stubborn. He's going to continue to make himself a nuisance until you tell him in no uncertain terms to back off. You're going to have to stay tough and not show any sign of weakness when he inevitably tries again."

Julie was suddenly ten years old again and her mother was berating her for mumbling or failing to make eye contact or not sticking up for herself when an older boy stole her lunch money. She wanted to curl into a ball and hide under the covers until the feeling passed.

"You're not helping, Greg," she said quietly. "In fact, you're making me feel worse."

His expression crumpled. "I'm sorry. That wasn't my intention. I just hate the way he treats you and I hate that I'm not here to help you."

"You *are* here to help me. You even threw an apple." She managed a sad smile. "And now I'm going wash his bowl and spoon and scrub away all traces of him."

"And call a locksmith tomorrow," Greg said. "I think it's time you changed the locks."

Julie added it to her mental list of things to do. For someone with no job and no one to look after, tomorrow was shaping up to be a busy day.

NINE

Monday brought with it a cloudless blue sky and a renewed sense of purpose for Julie. She left another voicemail for Howard, advising him to disregard her Saturday voicemail. She also called the locksmith about changing the locks and she received comparable estimates from the two roofers, selecting the one with the higher rating.

"Look at you go, Lady Boss," Greg said, as she set her phone on the kitchen counter.

Julie frowned at him. "Don't say Lady Boss. That's sexist."

Greg cringed. "If it's any consolation, as soon as I heard the words come out of my mouth, I wanted to take them back."

"It's okay. We've all suffered foot-in-mouth disease on occasion." She noticed he was wearing a different shirt today. "What happened to your Penn State T-shirt?"

He glanced at his outfit. "I guess I changed it."

"But how?"

"I don't know. I was wearing a hospital gown when I first became self-aware, but the next thing I knew I was wearing a T-shirt and jeans. Maybe it's because I complained."

Julie laughed. "Complained? Who are you—Ziggy? Is there some cosmic complaints desk where you file a form?"

"I didn't like my bare butt being exposed."

A thought occurred to her. "I bet that explains the woman I met in the hospital gown and the woman in the bunny slippers." Now that she thought about it, Barbara did mention it was the outfit she died in.

"You're seeing other ghosts?" Greg asked.

"It's not like I cheated on you. I didn't even know they were ghosts at the time. I thought I was hallucinating or something."

A smile tugged at the corners of his mouth. "You think seeing other ghosts constitutes cheating?"

"I didn't even know them," Julie said. "It was bizarre."

"What did they say?"

"They asked for my help." She tried to remember their conversations. "They said they were drawn to me."

Greg drifted over to gaze out the window. "Hey, it's snowing."

Julie joined him at the window. "It's only a dusting." It was only early January. They'd get a blizzard soon enough. Julie didn't look forward to shoveling. She'd have to hope the neighborhood kids came around looking for work.

"What are you going to do about the other ghosts?"

Julie blinked. "What do you mean?"

"They said they need your help. Maybe that's your gift—to be able to help them cross over."

Julie mulled it over. "Then why are you here when you'd already crossed over? Am I supposed to help you, too?"

Greg pulled a face. "You've got me there. No idea, but since you're not in a rush to get rid of me, why don't you contact the people you saw and deal with them first?"

"How? It's not like I can call them on the phone. They came to me."

"But they gave you information about themselves, right?"

Julie tried to remember what each apparition had told her. "I think so."

"Okay, then you should figure out what they need from you. It's probably the reason they're still here."

The woman in the bunny slippers was Barbara and her husband lived on Sycamore Road. "I'll start with Barbara. She gave me the most information."

A quick internet search revealed that Barbara Jean Honeywell died in her kitchen after slipping on a wet floor and hitting her head on the counter. An investigation determined that an ice cube had been dispensed from the refrigerator and fallen to the floor undetected, melting into a small puddle.

"That's unfortunate," Greg said, reading over Julie's shoulder.

"No more unfortunate than your death," she said. According to the article, Barbara died instantly. At least she didn't suffer, unlike Greg. Julie would never forgive the universe for causing her husband so much pain and discomfort in his final months of life.

"Her husband's name is Adam," Julie said. She craned her neck to look at Greg. "Do you think it would be weird for me to knock on the door and ask to talk to Barbara?"

"Yes," Greg said, "but I don't think you should let that stop you."

"Easy for you to say. You won't be the one taken to the psych ward."

"No, but I'd come visit you there. Being a ghost has its perks, like slipping past security without being seen."

Julie pretended to pat his cheek. "That's sweet of you."

"I'll come with you to Barbara's house. Make sure she doesn't chuck an apple at your head."

Julie bit back a smile. "And what will you do if she does?"

Greg looked thoughtful. "Guess I'd better level up on those poltergeist skills. If not for Barbara, then for Brad."

"Do you even know if it's possible to level up? Maybe an apple is your limit." Julie had visions of Greg trying to fly plates around the room and breaking them all in the process.

Greg inclined his head toward the computer. "I guess the internet isn't our best bet for this kind of research."

An idea bloomed. "No, but I know someone who might be able

to help. After Inga died, we met with Lorraine, a witch and self-proclaimed messenger to the spirit world."

"She sounds like a kook."

"I would've agreed with you before Inga died, but now I know better. Anyway, Lorraine tried to help us summon Inga's ghost, but it didn't work. She seemed to know a lot about the spirit world, though."

Julie checked the contacts in her phone and, sure enough, Lorraine's name was there.

"Okay then. Why don't we contact her first, before you start playing ghost whisperer?"

"I think we're overestimating the danger, but fine."

"Maybe so, but we're not overestimating your brother," Greg said pointedly.

Julie snickered. "Next time you can throw the whole fruit bowl at him."

"I'm serious, Julie. We don't know what his next move is, but I guarantee we haven't seen the last of him."

No, Julie agreed that Brad would be back for another round of pushing his sister around.

Lorraine answered on the first ring and Julie requested the next available appointment. The witch didn't ask for details. She simply told Julie to come in straight away. "Cash only," she added. "My card machine is on the fritz. Damn gremlins."

"Thanks, I'll be there shortly." Julie glanced at the bed and breakfast research on her computer screen. It seemed her own future would have to wait.

Julie was grateful the snow didn't stick. The backroads were narrow and winding and a scenic drive could easily turn treacherous in winter weather.

Lorraine's place of business was a small shop with a private room located at the back. Competing scents mingled in the air and Julie recognized rose and sage.

Lorraine, currently known as Soul Seer and formerly known as Messenger of the Spirits and the Voice of the Moon Goddess, wore a T-shirt emblazoned with *Witches Be Crazy* flanked by two dancing broomsticks. She paired the T-shirt with a floor-length skirt made from a crimson jacquard weave. Her hair was secured in a thick gray braid.

"Oh, right. The tall one," Lorraine said, sizing her up. "I wasn't sure which one of you was Julie. The only one I could remember was the blonde."

"Kate." No surprise there. Everybody remembered Kate.

"What brings you in? It's the beginning of the year, so I'm guessing a monthly forecast. What's your sign?"

Julie waved her off. "No, nothing like that. I have a situation."

Lorraine gave her an appraising look. "Step into my office."

"Are you sure this lady's legit?" Greg asked.

Julie ignored him and followed Lorraine into the back room. It wasn't the usual psychic setup. There was no scrying glass or beaded partition. The walls were tastefully decorated with framed black and white photographs of the phases of the moon. An Art Deco-style desk was positioned in the center of the room.

Lorraine gestured to a plush chair covered in purple velvet. "Take a load off your feet and your mind." She unscrewed a lid from a jar on her desk and offered it to Julie. "Marijuana gummy?"

"Uh, no thanks."

Greg made a disgruntled noise. "Where were those when I was sick?"

Lorraine popped one into her mouth and chewed. "You haven't come alone."

Julie straightened. "You can see him?"

"No, but I sense a presence." Her thick brows drew together. "Your husband?"

Julie nodded emphatically. "Yes!"

Lorraine replaced the lid and set the jar aside. "I take it you drank your cocktail."

"Yes, but that's not why I'm here."

"Oh, I think it is. You were finally ready to receive your gift and now you have questions." Lorraine flicked the end of her braid over her shoulder. "Is he the only ghost you've seen?"

Julie clasped her hands primly in her lap. "No. Ever since I drank the cocktail, ghosts have been drawn to me."

Lorraine didn't bat an eye at this revelation and Julie wondered how many ghosts Lorraine had seen in her lifetime. You couldn't call yourself a Messenger of the Spirits without a few ghost sightings under your belt.

"And you want to know how to make this stop?"

Julie hadn't considered that option. "Is that possible?"

"Nope. The magic is specific to the person, sweetie, and the universe has decided this is yours."

Julie wasn't sure how she felt about it. On the one hand, it meant Greg was here. On the other hand, it meant she was the flame to a bunch of ghostly moths. The prospect was unappealing, to say the least.

Lorraine plucked a pack of tarot cards from the side of the desk and began to shuffle. "If you're not here about your gift, then why are you here?"

"We'd like to know whether it's possible for Greg to become... less ghostly."

Lorraine's laugh was low and throaty. "You want a Pinocchio spell?"

"Pinocchio was a doll, not a ghost."

"I know, but he wanted to become real." Lorraine rolled her eyes. "Should I call it The Velveteen Rabbit spell? Would that make you happy?"

"That's still turning a toy into a real rabbit."

Lorraine narrowed her eyes. "Tough crowd." She cut the deck and shuffled again.

"He was able to move an apple and we want to know if there's a way for him to do even more, like opening and closing a door."

She frowned. "There's no need to open a door. He's a ghost. He can walk through walls."

Julie felt a flutter of annoyance. "Okay, that was just an example."

The older woman's eyes twinkled with amusement. "I thought your friend Kate is the one who likes to control things."

"I'm not trying to control anything." That was Doris's role, not Julie's.

"You're trying to manipulate your gift."

"I don't want to manipulate anything. I can interact with the physical world without help. It's Greg..."

Lorraine leaned forward across the desk and lowered her voice. "Surrender, honey. Dial down your Princess Leia resistance mantra and listen to what the universe is trying to tell you."

Greg snorted. "She made a *Star Wars* reference."

Julie shot him an aggrieved look before turning back to Lorraine. "The universe isn't telling me anything."

"I see." The older woman scraped a long purple nail against her cheek and Julie noticed it was the same deep purple as the chair. It seemed Lorraine had a favorite color.

"Can you help us?" Julie prompted.

"Yes, I think so."

Julie perked up. "Great! What do we have to do?"

"*We* don't have to do anything. Your husband should be able to develop this skill on his own."

Her expression crumpled. "It should come naturally? Because his hand goes right through everything. He was only able to move the apple because he was angry."

Lorraine shrugged. "Some spirits can throw things around right out of the gate. It depends on the person. If he works on focusing his energy, he should be able to manipulate objects at will. I don't mean he'll be driving a car, but he should certainly be able to flick a light switch off and on if you want to scare visitors."

Brad would hardly be scared by flickering lights and he was the only visitor she'd want to frighten.

Greg tried to rest a comforting hand on her shoulder but, as usual, he was unable to make contact and his hand simply disappeared.

"What about making him more solid?" Julie asked. "Is there a way we can make that happen?"

Lorraine scrutinized her. "You mean a resurrection?"

"Pretty sure my ashes take that option off the table," Greg said.

"Not a resurrection," Julie said. "I'm just wondering if there's a way to make him solid enough to hug."

Lorraine's eyes glinted in the dim light. "There might be a spell."

Julie's pulse raced. "One I could do?"

"It's possible you could perform it successfully, since your gift relates to spirits."

Julie and Greg exchanged looks of excitement.

"The spell brings a spirit into the physical plane," Lorraine continued.

"Have you ever done it?" Julie asked.

"No." Lorraine's lips tightened into a straight line. "I prefer to respect the division between realms."

Julie didn't care. If there was a sliver of a chance she could hug her husband one last time, she'd take it. "I'd like to try the spell."

Lorraine grunted. "I figured as much. I'll show you what you need in the shop."

"Wait, aren't you going to read my cards?" Julie gestured to the tarot cards on the desk that Lorraine had been shuffling.

The older woman glanced at the deck. "Oh, no. It's a stress reliever. Some people like to squeeze those rubber balls. I like to shuffle cards. I find it soothing." She rose from the chair and skirted the table to return to the shop. Picking up a basket, she swiveled to examine the assortment of items on the shelves.

Julie inhaled the aroma. "It smells good in this corner."

"It's all the dried herbs and flowers." She tapped her purple fingernail against her chin as she scanned the labels. "Right. Here we go. Elderberry, water lily, and Morning Glory." She placed each jar in the basket.

Julie raised her brow. "Morning Glory?"

Lorraine snickered. "Get your head out of the gutter. It's a flower."

Julie would have to ask Libbie and Kate if they'd heard of it. "What do the flowers do?"

"Elderberry signifies regeneration, renewal, and transformation." She continued to gather the ingredients. "A water lily symbolizes rebirth. In Egyptian mythology, there's a story about a sun god born from a water lily in order to light up the darkness in the world."

Greg's physical presence would certainly light up her dark world, no doubt about it.

"Morning Glory's real name is *Ipomoea purpurea*. According to Chinese folklore, these flowers bloom and die in one day."

"So they're the mayflies of the flower world," Julie said.

Lorraine snorted. "It's a little more romantic than that. For the Chinese, the flower symbolized the single day of the year when lovers who'd been separated by spiteful gods were able to meet."

Julie unscrewed the lid of the jar to inspect the dried flowers. "I can understand why this one's necessary."

"It's the lynchpin of the spell," Lorraine agreed. "Morning Glory is the belt and the other two are the suspenders."

"Got it." Julie replaced the lid and set the jar back in the basket. "I assume he doesn't have to drink anything, given that he doesn't have internal organs."

"No, you'll burn this mixture and let it mingle in the air with his spirit. It should give him solidity." Lorraine pinned her with a serious gaze. "Keep in mind, though, this is a Cinderella spell."

"I guess that makes her our fairy godmother," Greg joked.

"What does that mean?" Julie asked. "The spell wears off at midnight?"

"Not necessarily when the clock strikes twelve, but it most definitely ends."

Temporary or not, Julie was thrilled to have the option. "Thank you, Lorraine. This sounds perfect."

She gave Julie a set of written instructions. "You must follow these precisely. No improvisation. This isn't cooking with Emeril. You don't put your own spin on it."

"Like Libbie does with her cocktails?" As a chef, Libbie already had the right skill set, but with her newfound confidence, she was now a wiz with creative magical recipes.

"This is not a cocktail. This is a different sort of magic," she advised. "You don't want to end up with a zombie."

Julie's eyes popped. "A zombie? Is that even possible?"

Lorraine shifted her gaze to the shelf. "Let's just say that not all fiction comes from the imagination."

Julie contemplated the instructions. "And this won't hurt Greg, right?"

The older woman gave her a hard look. "You do remember he's already dead."

"I know, but I don't want this to...send him back to where he came from or somewhere worse."

Lorraine exhaled gently. "It won't do you any good to kid yourself. He'll go back to where he came from eventually, one way or another."

Julie wasn't convinced. If she could see ghosts now, why not have Greg stay until she withered and died, too? They could still live a life together, however unconventional.

"How long will we have?" Julie asked.

Lorraine pursed her lips. "Maybe six to eight hours, tops. I wouldn't plan a transatlantic trip, or if you do, don't buy him his own seat."

"Thank you for your help," Julie said. "We really appreciate it."

"Best of luck, Jenny."

Julie didn't bother to correct her. The only thing she cared about was that she had the ingredients for a spell that would make Greg whole again. Two hours. Six. Julie didn't mind how long the spell lasted. It was a second chance and she couldn't wait to take full advantage of it. The only decision left to make was when.

TEN

Julie parked in front of the house on Sycamore Road. Despite the presence of her ghostly husband, she felt ridiculous for coming to a stranger's house and trying to—what exactly? Julie didn't know how to handle such a delicate situation. What if the husband was unhinged?

They'd spent hours after their visit to Lorraine trying to agree on the best time to perform the spell. Julie had wanted to use it the minute they arrived home, but Greg's approach was more cautious. He wanted to understand more about their situation first. Finally, they agreed to wait and see what happened after Julie 'helped' the other ghosts she'd met. Neither one was entirely certain what her help would entail, but she was eager to get started. As far as Julie was concerned, the sooner she helped ghosts cross over or whatever it was they needed, the sooner she and Greg could focus on each other.

"What's your plan?" Greg asked. "Knock on the door and tell the husband you want to summon his dead wife?"

Julie glared at him. "No. I figured I'd stand in the yard and call to her. She's probably lingering around the house."

"If she has any sense of fun, she'll be downtown spying on people."

"Not everyone is as nosy as you." She opened the car door and walked around to the side of the house to see if there was any sign of the woman in the bunny slippers.

"She's more likely inside the house than hanging out in the backyard in the middle of winter," Greg said.

"I was in my yard when she accosted me," Julie said, a tad defensive. "Barbara," Julie called in a loud whisper. "Barbara, can you hear me? I'm here to help you."

Greg scoped the area. "I don't see anyone, except the neighbor across the street peeping out her window."

"Oh, that's Myrtle."

Julie jumped at the sound of Barbara's voice.

"She's as nosy as they come," Barbara continued. "I once caught her poking through our mailbox when she thought we weren't home. She claimed she was searching for a letter that got misdelivered." Barbara rolled her eyes. "Yeah, right."

Julie tried to quell the nerves fluttering in her stomach. "Hi, Barbara. I'm sorry about last time. If it's okay with you, I'd like to help you with your issue now. I just need to know what it is."

Barbara's face split into a grin. "I'm so glad." Her gaze shifted to Greg. "Who's this?"

"My husband, Greg."

He offered his hand and then seemed to remember he was incorporeal.

Barbara's mouth formed a thin line. "Would you mind? This is a private matter."

Julie cut him a sidelong glance. "I'll catch up with you later."

"Are you sure?" he asked. "What if this goes sideways?"

Julie laughed. "It's not a job for the mob." She paused and looked at Barbara. "Right?"

"No, it's a personal matter."

Greg's ghostly form dissipated, leaving Julie alone with Barbara.

"I'm sorry I was unhelpful last time," Julie said. "I didn't know what was happening."

Barbara waved her off. "It's no problem. I'm just glad you came looking for me. I wasn't sure what else to do. I can't seem to go anywhere outside the town line. I get pulled straight back to the house."

"What is it you think I can do for you?" Julie asked.

Barbara inclined her head toward the backyard. "I need you to get something for me."

Something in the backyard? "You didn't bury anyone, did you, Barbara? Because I'm not digging up any bodies. I don't have the upper body strength for it." Or the stomach.

"It's nothing like that. I hid something that belongs to my husband and I need you to put it back in the house so he can find it."

"What is it?"

"An autographed baseball. He got it as a kid during the 1980 World Series when the Phillies won."

"Wow. So it's his prized possession."

"Oh, completely. Why do you think I took it in the first place?"

"You must've really wanted to make a point."

Barbara slid a coy look in my direction. "I had a tendency to fight dirty."

"You don't think he'll find it without your help?"

"No way. He's been looking everywhere in the house, but he'd never think to look in the yard."

"Did you bury it?"

"No, I wasn't one for manual labor. I hid it in the bushes behind the shed."

"Do you mind if I ask why?"

"Why do you think? Because I was mad at him. I didn't expect to die before I could return it to him, now did I?" She flicked a glance at the house. "He's been driving himself crazy, obsessing over it. I think, in part, as a way of coping with my death."

Julie realized she'd been too busy dealing with her mother to process her own grief. No wonder she had trouble moving forward. She hadn't been permitted time to mourn. Doris had kept her busy, especially in those early days. If she sensed Julie was wallowing, she'd bark out orders to scrub the oven or pull the weeds in the garden. Julie gave her mother more pedicures than she cared to count.

"What got you so worked up that you hid the ball in the first place?" Julie asked.

"It's stupid, really. I caught him checking out another woman and I went ballistic."

"You think he was cheating?"

"Oh, no. Not at all." Barbara tucked a strand of hair behind her ear. "You know how it is, though. You hit middle age and suddenly you're invisible. Men don't notice you anymore. The thing is, the young woman was stunning. A real head turner." Barbara shook her head. "But I'd been feeling bloated and miserable and when I saw the way he looked at her..." She trailed off. "I wanted him to look that way at me. His wife."

For a fleeting moment, Julie thought the woman might cry, but Barbara held herself together.

"I overreacted because of my own insecurities. I know he would never cheat." She laughed. "Not that a gorgeous young woman would have any interest in my middle-aged lump of a husband." Her eyes grew damp. "That's what I called him sometimes—Lumpy. I know it sounds mean, but it was a term of endearment, honestly."

"No judgment," Julie said, holding up her hands.

"The key is to let him think he found the ball on his own," Barbara said. "I think he could use that sense of achievement. He's barely made it into the shower lately."

Barbara guided her to a spot in the backyard behind the shed and pointed to the bushes where a flash of white caught her eye.

"At least you didn't bury it," Julie said, scooping up the ball. "The ground would be too frozen to dig it up."

Barbara regarded her. "A little shovel action might do you some good. Maybe you should think about investing in a set of hand weights."

"Hey," Julie said defensively. "I'm doing you a favor. I don't need the fitness critique."

"They'll do wonders for your muscles and bone density."

"Oh, you're a medical expert now that you're dead?"

She squared her shoulders. "I was a dental hygienist."

"Congratulations."

Barbara waved her forward. "Come on. I'll show you where to put the ball."

"You're sure he won't be home anytime soon?"

"Not until six. Plenty of time. The key to the back door is in the birdhouse."

She followed Barbara to the back door and removed the key. "This is a good hiding spot. Which room am I going to?"

"His man cave downstairs is a mess. I think it's our best bet."

"How will he find the ball if the room's a mess?"

"I'll nudge him in the right direction. I couldn't exactly nudge him to the yard behind the shed. Too tricky."

Julie unlocked the back door and stepped inside the kitchen. "Where's the staircase?"

Barbara crooked a finger. "This way."

Julie trailed behind her as they reached an open doorway.

"I used to resent that he took over the entire lower level. The joke's on me, though. The whole house is his man cave now," Barbara lamented as they descended the stairs.

The moment Julie's foot landed on the floor, she realized this whole exercise had been a lapse in judgment. A man stood in the center of the room wearing a virtual reality headset, red boxer shorts, and nothing else. His hands were occupied by two controllers.

Julie glared at Barbara. "You said he wouldn't be home." She should've realized when Barbara said he'd be out until six that it wasn't true. If he was having trouble making it to the shower, odds were good he'd be home.

Barbara shrugged. "I lied, sue me. I figured you'd refuse to help if you knew you'd have to talk to him."

"With good reason! He could have a gun and shoot me," Julie said in a harsh whisper.

Barbara blew a dismissive breath. "We don't own guns."

Julie turned to head back up the steps, but Barbara reacted quickly by knocking over a discarded mug that sat on top of a tower of crates. The mug crashed to the floor.

"Hey, what do you think you're doing?"

Julie froze, uncertain what to do. Slowly, she turned to face Barbara's husband. He'd removed the headset and controllers, and was more concerned with Julie's presence than his half naked state.

"Um, my name is Julie Duncan."

"His name is Adam," Barbara said softly.

"Why are you whispering?" Julie asked. "He can't hear you."

"Exactly. That's why you're here. To be my voice."

Julie didn't know how Barbara expected her to act as a voice for a complete stranger when Julie didn't even use her voice for herself.

Adam's brow creased as he observed Julie. "Who are you talking to?" The frown lines deepened when he spotted the ball in Julie's hand. "Hey, is that my baseball? I've been looking every-where for that."

Barbara motioned for Julie to walk closer.

"It is," Julie said. She held out the ball for him to take it. "It was in the bushes behind the shed."

Reluctantly, Adam took the ball and inspected it. "I don't understand."

"Barbara put the ball in the bushes to hide it from you."

Adam's head snapped up and his eyes locked with Julie's. "Excuse me? When did she tell you that?"

"Today," Julie said. She inhaled deeply. "She's standing next to me right now."

Adam's eyes turned to slits and his nostrils flared. "Who hired you? Is this some kind of sick joke?"

Julie didn't think she'd ever felt so uncomfortable in her life. She made a point of avoiding confrontation and now she was smack in the middle of one with complete strangers. She forced herself to get the conversation over with.

"Barbara was angry with you before she died and she hid the ball to get back at you. She's not proud…"

"Well, I'm a little proud," Barbara interrupted. "It was a good hiding spot."

Julie turned to gape at the ghost. "Priorities, Barbara." She switched her gaze back to Adam. "Anyway, she wants you to know she's sorry and asked that I bring the ball back so you can stop tearing apart the house."

Adam hefted the ball in his hand. "She told you this before she died?"

"No, Adam. I told you—she's standing next to me now."

He looked to Julie's left and she hooked a thumb to her right to redirect him.

Adam clenched his jaw. "I don't believe you."

Julie cut a sideways glance at Barbara. "I gave him the ball. Can I go now?" If the ball was Barbara's unfinished business, then she'd be gone soon enough. Julie wanted to be out of there before Adam decided to call the police and report a deranged intruder.

Barbara grew wistful as she looked at her husband. "Not yet. Tell him I'm sorry."

"I already told him."

She shook her head. "Not about the ball. Tell him I'm sorry about vet school, too."

Vet school? Barbara's pitiful expression tugged at Julie's heartstrings and she cleared her throat. "She wants you to know she's sorry about vet school."

His mouth dropped open. "What are you? Some kind of psychic?"

"More like a ghost whisperer," Julie said. "Barbara came to me about the ball and tricked me into coming down here. She told me you wouldn't be home and I could just put the ball down here and leave."

To her relief, he chuckled. "That sounds like Barbara. My

friends called her puppet master because she was always pulling everybody's strings to get her way."

Barbara beamed proudly. "I was somewhat of a master."

"What was the deal with vet school?" Julie asked.

Barbara smiled tenderly at her husband. "About ten years ago, he said he wanted to change careers and go to vet school. I said no, that he was too old and we couldn't afford it." She cupped her cheeks with her hands. "God, I'm so selfish. I wouldn't even let him have a pet."

"Not even a cat?" Julie asked.

Adam stared in disbelief. "No, not even a cat." He hesitated. "What else is she saying?"

"You should get a dog now," Barbara said. "Tell him he should have one of those Great Danes he always wanted. I didn't want a big dog, or any dog."

"She says you should have a Great Dane," Julie repeated.

Tears streamed down his cheeks. "It's really her."

"It really is." Julie fished a clean tissue from her purse and handed one to him. "I'm sorry for your loss."

Adam used the tissue to wipe away his tears and blow his nose. "How does she look? Does she look like herself or is she more like a walking skeleton with maggots coming out of empty eye sockets?"

Julie scrunched her nose in disgust as the image formed in her mind.

"He loves virtual games," Barbara said, by way of explanation. "A little too much these days, as you can see from the state of this place."

Julie's gaze swept the room and she took in the overloaded shelves and the empty plates and mugs scattered across the available surfaces. Adam seemed to have been neglecting everything in favor of living in an alternate reality—a place where skeletons roamed the earth with maggots in their eye sockets, apparently.

"She's beautiful," Julie said. "I can see why you fell in love with her."

"And now tell him it's time to find someone new," Barbara announced.

Julie recoiled. "Wait. What?"

Barbara pressed on. "There's that pretty blonde who lives down the road. She's a solid candidate. She runs past here most days around six. It would be easy to bump into her."

Julie's eyes widened slightly. "You're actively shopping for your replacement? You were so mad about him looking at another woman that you hid his prized possession and now you're putting him on the market?"

"I'm dead now, Julie," she said. "Needs and wants are only for the living."

"What?" Adam asked. "What are you talking about?"

Julie wasn't sure whether to share this part. It seemed too personal. Then again, in for a penny, in for a pound.

"Tell him," Barbara said. "It's important."

Julie suddenly realized that *this* was the reason Barbara was still here and the reason she sought out Julie. Not for Adam's baseball or vet school. Not for Adam's past but his future.

"You really won't mind if he starts dating?" Julie asked.

"Honey, I'm dead. Why would I mind? I love him. I want the big lump to be happy, not sitting around in his boxers in the basement for decades like a testosterone-fueled Miss Havisham."

Julie stood in awe of Barbara. "Your wife says there's a pretty blonde who lives down the street who runs past here most days."

"She wears those shiny leggings," Barbara added.

Adam nodded. "The one in the shiny leggings."

Barbara smirked. "See? I knew he noticed her."

"Barbara thinks you should ask her out," Julie said.

"Kelly," Adam said. "That's her name. I met her last year at a neighborhood barbecue."

"Remind him she eats meat," Barbara said. "I'm a vegetarian and that always added stress to mealtimes. Adam likes a good steak."

"Kelly eats meat, apparently," Julie said.

Adam's whole face brightened. "That's right. She was next to me in line for a burger."

Barbara glided closer to him. "You have a lot of years left to enjoy, Adam. I don't want you to spend them alone or waste them in some alternate reality." She tried to brush a stray hair from his forehead, but her fingers sliced through the air. "You're a good man, and I am so blessed to have met you."

"Do you want me to translate any of this?" Julie asked, feeling awkward to be privy to such a private moment.

Adam glanced at Julie. "What's she saying?"

Barbara kept her focus on her husband. "Tell him to lay off the VR and rejoin civilization. My orders."

Julie repeated the command and he smiled. "She's still pulling my strings from beyond the grave. I guess I shouldn't be surprised." He fixed Julie with a curious look. "Does this mean I'll be able to talk to her through you whenever I want?"

Barbara shook her head sadly. "It's the end of the road for us, I'm afraid, but you know what they say—when a vegetarian door closes, a carnivorous one opens."

Julie swallowed hard. "Barbara is here to say goodbye."

Adam flinched. "But I don't want to say goodbye. She only just got here."

"She's been with you," Julie said, "and that's why she's concerned. She wants you to live your life to the fullest and not squander the time you've been given."

He scratched the back of his neck in a thoughtful gesture. "She really wants me to get to know Kelly, huh?"

Barbara swiveled to look at Julie. "Tell him I insist."

"She insists."

Adam's head bobbed up and down as he digested the order. "I can't promise she'll be as gullible as you and fall head over heels in love with me, but I'll see if I can work the old Adam magic."

"Tell him to throw away the socks with holes in them." She waved a finger, remembering more instructions. "And don't wear that horrible cologne that your mom bought. It makes you smell like you showered in acid."

"I think we're done here, Barbara," Julie said.

Barbara pursed her lips. "I'm going to miss you more than you'll ever know." She turned back to Julie. "I'm sorry about tricking you."

"It's okay," Julie said. "I understand. Good luck to both of you." She wasn't sure if it made sense to wish Barbara luck, but she felt the need to say *something*.

"If you don't mind, I'd like to spend my final moments alone with my husband."

"Of course. It was nice meeting you, Adam," Julie said with a wave.

"Thank you!" he called after her.

She hurried up the steps to avoid watching Barbara say good-bye. The pain was too sharp, poking her in places that she thought long buried. By the time she left the house, she was in tears. She slid behind the wheel with a blotchy face and a trembling chin, prompting a look of concern from Greg.

"Everything okay?" he asked.

She dabbed at her eyes with a tissue. "Everything's fine."

"Doesn't look fine. Looks like you just found out your husband died."

Julie knew it was a joke, but she wasn't in the mood to humor him. She started the car and kept her gaze forward.

"Do we need to wait for Barbara?" he asked.

Wordlessly, she shook her head and pulled out of the driveway. If she opened her mouth to answer, she knew a torrent of emotions would push their way out and she wasn't prepared to deal with it. Not now. And maybe not ever.

ELEVEN

Julie stood in the backyard with Jed, the young roofer she hired. Her neck was starting to cramp from being tilted back too long as Jed explained what the problem was and what he did to repair it. Julie appreciated that he didn't talk down to her or try to mansplain. For a twenty-five-year-old, he seemed to have a good head on his shoulders and Julie was glad she'd chosen him to do the work.

"Great job, Jelly. You handled that like a pro," Greg said, once Jed had returned to his truck.

"Thanks." It felt good to cross a big job off the list.

"What else is on our agenda today?" Greg asked. "B&B research or ghost hunting?"

She arched a skeptical eyebrow. "Oh, it's *our* agenda, is it?"

"I can go haunt the downtown area if you'd rather be on your own. I think the cashier at the deli might be stealing singles from the register."

"I'd much rather spend time with you—you know that, but I think I should find the other ghosts so I can help them go into the light or whatever. Then I can focus my attention on the only ghost that really matters."

"Aw, that's sweet. Are you sure you don't want me to go with you?" he asked.

"Actually, I'm going to ask Rebecca since she knew this woman and I think there's a dog involved." She remembered that Rosie had asked that she talk to the dog and assure her everything would be okay.

Greg nodded. "Mind if I take off for a bit then?"

"Go for it, Casper."

"Haunt you later," Greg said with a cheerful wink and disappeared.

Julie entered the house and called Rebecca. "I need to know where Millie lives," she said.

"Who's Millie?"

"The older dog that was adopted from the shelter."

"Oh, Rosie's dog. Her name is Mollie. I thought you were talking about a person."

"Rosie needs me to do something for the dog." Now that Julie had a better understanding of what was happening, she knew it meant honoring Rosie's request.

"I guess that makes sense. Rosie was devoted to Mollie."

"Will you come with me?" Julie wasn't experienced with dogs and she'd feel better with an expert by her side.

"Of course. You don't need to worry. Mollie's a sweetheart. You'll see."

Julie collected Rebecca from her house first so they could ride to the apartment building together.

"How do we know the dog is still in Rosie's apartment?" Rebecca asked, once they were en route. "Can you sense that?"

"No, but I think I'm more likely to make contact with Rosie there and she can tell us."

"Tell me what?"

Julie gasped at the sight of the old woman in the rearview mirror. "Rosie, how did you...? Forget it." She was a ghost. A moving vehicle was no obstacle.

Rebecca cast a sidelong glance at Julie. "Rosie's here?"

Rosie noticed Rebecca in the passenger seat. "Oh, terrific. A reunion. Tell Rebecca I really like her hair."

"Rosie likes your hair."

Rebecca turned and smiled in the direction of the back seat. "Thanks. I colored it over the weekend."

"I gave up on all that nonsense," Rosie said. "At some point, you just need to embrace how you look."

Julie wasn't quite ready to embrace a head of silver hair. Maybe in another twenty years, she'd feel differently.

"How did you know to come back to me?" Julie asked.

"I don't know," Rosie said. "I felt a weird pull and then poof! Here I am in your car." She patted the seat. "Nice comfy interior. I've always preferred cloth to leather. Where are we headed?"

"Your apartment to find Mollie," Julie said.

"Oh, she isn't there."

Julie groaned. "Where is she?"

"My friend Ira took her in. Same building. Different apartment."

Okay, that wasn't so bad. "What is it that you need me to do?" Julie asked.

Rosie hesitated. "Rebecca isn't going to like it."

That sounded ominous. "Why not?"

"Mollie's an old dog. She was old when I adopted her. I saw her at the shelter and thought, yep. These two old broads deserve each other."

Julie smiled at the rearview mirror.

"Some places can be strict about who can adopt—between my age and my apartment, I was worried they wouldn't let me have her, but Rebecca was thrilled when I said I wanted her."

"How many years were you together?" Julie asked.

"Seven." Rosie's expression clouded over. "Mollie helped me through so many difficult times. She was my best friend." Her eyes brimmed with unshed tears. "I hate that she's suffering."

Julie's eyebrows shot up. "Suffering?"

Rebecca's head jerked toward her. "Who's suffering?"

"Let's just get to the apartment," Julie said. She didn't want to upset her friend, too. She knew how strongly Rebecca felt about animals.

"Turn left here," Rosie said.

Julie glanced at the map on her dashboard. "The GPS says it's two more blocks."

"It's a shortcut."

Julie swerved in time to make the turn and narrowly missed hitting a sign. "What's next?"

Rosie peered out the window. "Hmm. This doesn't look familiar. I think I might've been wrong. Go back to the road you were on."

Julie bit her tongue. The woman was dead and her dog was suffering. There was no point in getting worked up over a wrong turn. She simply pulled into the nearest driveway and turned around.

"What's going on?" Rebecca asked.

"Wrong turn," Julie said. "I'll follow the GPS from now on if that's okay with you, Rosie."

"I'm surprised you listened to me at all," Rosie said. "Nobody listens to old women. We could have all the wisdom in the universe, but no one would know it because they don't ask."

"Do you have all the wisdom in the universe?" Julie asked.

Rosie blew a raspberry. "Who do I look like—Stephen Hawking? Of course not. I just told you to turn on the wrong street, for Pete's sake."

Julie drew a cleansing breath and followed the GPS until they reached the apartment building.

"Ira lives in 3B," Rosie said.

The three women entered the building and made their way to 3B.

"Hey, I can take the stairs instead of the elevator," Rosie declared. "Another perk of being a ghost." She looked around the stairwell. "I always worried someone would murder me in a stairwell, but it's not too scary in here."

Julie laughed. "Do you think men ever worry about things like that?"

"About what?" Rebecca asked.

"Walking through a parking lot alone at night. Jogging before the sun comes up. Walking alone in a stairwell." Julie pushed open the door to the third floor. "Any of it, really."

"Of course not. It's an entire survival mindset we learn from an early age," Rebecca said.

"I'd love to haunt some of those jackasses," Rosie said.

"Maybe that can be next on the list," Julie said.

They arrived at 3B and Julie knocked on the door.

"If you can keep Ira occupied," she told Rebecca, "that would be great."

After a prolonged moment, an elderly man answered the door. He was mostly bald, with only a few tufts of gray hair remaining above his ears. He wore a black long-sleeved top with gray chinos and moccasin slippers on his feet.

"He's still wearing those slippers?" Rosie made a disgruntled noise. "I told him after Thanksgiving to get rid of them. There's a hole in the toe that lets in the cold air. Men are so lazy."

Julie ignored her and focused on Ira. "Hi. My name is Julie Duncan and this is my friend, Rebecca Angelos. We were hoping to have a short visit with Mollie. We understand you've been caring for her ever since Rosie died."

Ira's face registered surprise. "Yes, of course."

Another man appeared behind Ira. He was taller and about twenty-five years younger than Ira, with a full head of brown hair and an attractive smile. In fact, everything about him was attractive. Julie quickly squelched the uncomfortable thought.

"Hi. I'm Ira's son, David."

"David's a doctor," Rosie said.

"Nice to meet you." Julie shook his hand. It was a nice grip, firm but not too tight.

"No need to stand in the hall," Ira said. "Come on in." He shuffled over to the sofa and sat down. "Don't mind me. My knees are bothering me today. David came by to check on me."

"Did you know Rosie?" David asked.

Julie was grateful when Rebecca intercepted the question. "We met at the shelter where I work. That's where she adopted Mollie."

David eyed her closely. "I thought you looked familiar. I adopted my dog from there, too. Maybe you remember him. A mixed breed called Bailey."

Rebecca pointed at him, remembering. "Part Schnauzer."

David broke into a wide smile. "That's him. He's a great dog."

"If I recall correctly, your girlfriend didn't seem as excited as you. I hope she's come around." Although she phrased it as a statement, there was the hint of a question in Rebecca's voice.

"Well, she's not my girlfriend anymore," David said.

"And good riddance to bad rubbish," Ira chimed in from the sofa.

David glanced over his shoulder. "She wasn't that bad, Dad." He turned back to the women. "We didn't see eye-to-eye on a few things that turned out to be deal breakers for me."

"And the dog was one of them, I gather," Rebecca said.

"I could've told you that," Rosie said. "The woman never so much as looked in Mollie's direction when she passed us. She barely acknowledged me either, and I'd met her a dozen times."

Julie caught sight of the shorthaired terrier curled up on a small bed in the corner of the room. She seemed to be asleep, but as Julie approached, the dog lifted her head, fully alert.

"Mind if I talk to the dog?" Julie asked.

"Be my guest," Ira said.

"This is a lovely apartment," Rebecca said, in an effort to keep Ira and David distracted.

Julie and Rosie ventured to the corner of the room to see Mollie.

"There's my girl," Rosie said. She drifted over to sit on the floor beside the dog bed. "One of the perks of being dead is no arthritis. I can get up and down without twenty joints screaming at me."

Mollie seemed to sense Rosie's presence, although it was unclear whether the dog could see her former companion. After all, Mollie wasn't a witch's companion.

"Do you think she can hear you?" Julie whispered.

Rosie tried to scratch behind Mollie's ear. "I don't think so. That's why I need you."

Julie scratched the same spot so the dog could feel it. "You talk and I'll scratch."

"Rub her belly, too," Rosie said. "She likes that."

Julie stroked the terrier's back. She wasn't going to roll the dog over unless Mollie indicated she wanted that.

"You're such a good girl," Rosie said in a soothing tone.

"Thanks," Julie replied.

Rosie glared at her. "I'm talking to the dog."

"Oh, right." Julie continued her role as dog petter.

"I know you're in pain," Rosie said. "Believe me, I've been there, but I want you to know that it's okay to let go. It's safe where I am and we'll see each other again when you get there, I promise. It'll be liver treats and squeaky toys to your heart's content."

The dog panted and slowly rolled onto her back. Julie patted her belly as Rosie continued to talk.

"Ira will be fine, so don't worry about leaving him. He was a good friend to take you in after I died. I shouldn't have asked him, really, but I didn't know what else to do. I was worried you'd end up..." Rosie cut herself off. "You're my little sweetheart and I love you."

Julie's chest tightened. There was clearly a strong connection between Rosie and the dog. "Do you want me to repeat all that?" she whispered.

"Do your best," Rosie said. "I'm sure you won't be as eloquent, but beggars can't be choosers."

Julie glared at her. "Gee, thanks." She leaned down to whisper in the dog's ear.

"She's been lethargic," Ira said, wandering over to check on them. "David and I took her to the vet, but she couldn't find anything wrong. She said it's old age and told us to keep her comfortable and make sure she's eating and drinking."

"She has a tumor," Rosie said. "The vet missed it, but it doesn't matter. Mollie's too old. She wouldn't survive the treatment."

Julie wondered about the old woman's plan. Did she want Julie to tell Ira about the tumor? It didn't sound like it.

"You were a good friend to Rosie," Julie said. "She would've really appreciated you taking care of Mollie."

Ira pulled out a handkerchief and dabbed at his eyes. "I still can't believe Rosie's gone. It doesn't matter how old I get, I'm always surprised when someone leaves us."

David came over to place a comforting hand on his dad's shoulder. "Because you still think you're thirty."

"Only on the inside," Ira said. "Sometimes I catch a glimpse of myself in the mirror and think 'who in the hell is that old man in my bathroom?'"

David chuckled. "You look great, Dad."

Rosie smiled up at him. "I miss you, old friend."

Rebecca crouched beside Julie to pet the dog. "Has she been eating normally?"

"Not really," Ira said. "Enough to keep her going maybe."

Rebecca studied the dog. "She had so much energy for an older dog. I remember worrying whether it might be too much for Rosie to handle."

"Ha!" Rosie said. "Not likely."

Julie couldn't talk to Rosie with everyone standing close by. She caught the ghost's eye and gave her a questioning look.

"Just a little longer," Rosie said, her expression solemn.

Julie continued to speak to Mollie in a soothing tone.

"Can I get anyone a drink?" Ira offered. "Or should I say, can David get anyone a drink?"

David smiled. "I'm happy to play the role of host. We have tea or coffee."

"I'm somewhat of an herbal tea aficionado," Ira said. "If you can dream it, I've probably got a sachet of it."

"That's a bold statement," Rebecca said.

"Nothing for me, thanks," Julie said. Her gaze remained fixed on the dog.

"How about you, Dad?" David asked. "I can make you something before I go."

Ira rubbed his hands up and down his thighs. "I think I'm in the mood for honey and lavender today."

"Sounds perfect for a cold day," Rebecca said, smiling at him.

It didn't escape Julie's attention that Mollie's breathing had slowed considerably. Rosie cradled the dog's head and whispered encouraging words. Finally, the old woman raised her head and looked at Julie.

"She's crossed the rainbow bridge," Rosie said.

Julie's gaze swept the room. Would she see Mollie's ghost, too? "Are you sure?" she whispered.

"I can feel it." Rosie lowered her head and brushed her lips across the dog's snout. "I'll see you soon, friend."

"Rebecca," Julie whispered. "Mollie's no longer with us."

Rebecca gave the dog an affectionate pat on the head. "Sweet dreams, Mollie." She returned to a standing position. "Ira, I have bad news. I'm afraid Mollie has decided to join Rosie."

Ira didn't appear surprised by the news. "They'll be reunited. That's something."

It was more than something. As far as Julie was concerned, it was everything.

David ducked back into the living room. "I'm so glad you were here." He paused. "Well, I'm not glad you had to be here when she died, of course, but I'm glad she was surrounded by people who care about her. A lot of humans aren't that fortunate."

"He would know," Rosie said. "Did I mention he's a doctor?"

Rosie would know, too, Julie realized. She'd died alone in the hospital. Julie wondered whether that was part of the reason she'd stuck around—because she didn't want Mollie to suffer a similar fate.

"I'd be happy to make the arrangements for Mollie," Rebecca said. "It's sort of in my wheelhouse."

"I already told Ira what I want for Mollie," Rosie interrupted.

"I appreciate that," Ira said, "but I know what to do. Rosie gave me explicit instructions and I know better than to circumvent her wishes. She'd probably come back to haunt me and I won't risk that."

"Damn straight," Rosie said. "You're a good man, Ira. I was lucky to know you."

It was clear the two older people had enjoyed a close friendship. Julie wondered whether there'd been anything more between them.

Julie reluctantly stood and walked away from the dog. Although she knew it was the right time for Mollie to go, she still felt sad. It occurred to her that humans had a complicated relationship with death.

"Thanks for visiting Mollie," Ira said. "Rosie would be pleased to know the dog had extra support when she passed."

The women headed toward the door. "It was lovely to meet you," Rebecca said.

David joined them at the door and offered Julie a warm smile. "Thanks for stopping by. It was really kind of you."

"He's got great abs," Rosie said, as they returned to the stairwell. "I saw him come out of the shower once by accident when he was staying with Ira."

They walked the rest of the way to the car in silence. Although Julie was surprised that Rosie was still with them, she didn't mind. The older woman seemed like good company.

Only after they dropped off Rebecca did Julie turn to give Rosie an accusatory look. "You knew Ira's son would be there, didn't you?"

Rosie shrugged. "How could I? I didn't know when you'd be stopping by."

Julie still felt as though Rosie had somehow planned the meeting with David. "I'm married, Rosie."

"You're a widow. That's not the same as being married."

Julie's eyes narrowed. "How do you know?"

"I'm a ghost. I haunt and I know things."

"Well, it just so happens that my husband is also a ghost and we're making it work."

Rosie snorted. "You're making it work, are you? Now there's a show I'd like to watch."

"We're happy together," Julie said. "It isn't ideal, but what relationship is?"

"Listen to yourself." Rosie shook her head. "Sweetheart, face it. Your husband is dead and he's never coming back, not in any meaningful way."

"It's meaningful to me."

Rosie tried to cover Julie's hand with her own. "You need to let him go, honey. Trust me. The only way is forward."

"It's easy for you to say. You told Mollie to let go because it means you'll be reunited soon. If I let Greg go..." She trailed off.

Rosie glowered at her. "You think I encouraged Mollie to let go for selfish reasons? She was clinging to life out of fear. It was a kindness, Julie. An act of love."

"An act that just happens to benefit you," Julie shot back. She wasn't sure why she felt irritated by the old woman, but she did.

"David is a catch," Rosie said. "His last girlfriend was all flash and no substance. He needs more than that."

"Well, I don't need David, but thanks for thinking of me."

"He seemed interested. He gave you that charming smile. He doesn't give that to everyone, you know."

"That's nice."

"Is that your final answer?" Rosie asked.

"Why? Because you won't ask again?"

Rosie glanced outside at the scenery. "Because this is my stop."

"Your stop?"

"I did what I needed to do. Now it's time to go and be with Mollie again."

Julie felt guilty for giving Rosie a hard time. "You mean you're leaving for good."

"That's how it works. My unfinished business is done and dusted. I was trying to sneak in a little extra project before the door hit me in the ass, but if you're not interested, I won't force the issue. I like to offer suggestions, but I'm not browbeating anybody into a decision they're not ready to make."

A feeling of tenderness washed over Julie. Why couldn't her own mother have been more like Rosie? There was no point in wishing for the impossible, not that it mattered anymore. Doris was dead and the next phase of Julie's life had begun. It was up to her to decide how she wanted to live it without the fear of criticism hanging over her.

"I'm so glad to have met you, Rosie," Julie said.

"Same here. A shame we didn't get to know each other when I was alive. I think we would've been friends." Rosie's form began to glow with a soft, white light. "If you're determined to stick it out with that ghost of a husband, you might want to consider investing in a vibrator. Just sayin.'"

And with those words of wisdom, Rosie disappeared.

TWELVE

Julie was grateful when Friday rolled around again. She was more than ready for an evening of cocktails and conversation with her friends. She was eager to tell them about recent events in greater detail and get their input on the bed and breakfast idea. They'd been her support system for as long as she'd known them and she knew they would offer solid advice as well as the encouragement she needed.

"There's something I've been meaning to tell you," Greg said, on the drive over to Rebecca's house.

"You're not actually dead?" she joked.

"That's wishful thinking—for both of us." He hesitated. "When you were with Rebecca, I went to check on Brad."

"And?" Julie kept her eyes on the road. Like many normal activities, nighttime driving had become increasingly difficult with age.

"He was on his laptop in the motel room, researching wills."

Her stomach plummeted. "You mean researching how to contest one."

"How, when, why—all the basics."

Julie was disappointed but not surprised. Her brother had always been stubborn. "Did he call a lawyer?"

"I didn't see any sign that he had, but it doesn't mean he won't."

Julie gripped the steering wheel. "Good thing it's cocktail club night." If anything could help her digest the news, it was a fun evening with her friends.

"I'm sorry. I considered not telling you because I didn't want to upset you, but I thought you should know. Forewarned is forearmed and all that."

She parked the car in the driveway behind Kate's SUV and smiled at him. "Thanks. I'm glad you told me."

Rebecca's house was situated on a hillside on the outskirts of town. The compact house was charming, with white siding, black shutters, and a front door a deep crimson color. Cheerful flower boxes underlined the first-floor windows and Rebecca had added Christmas cacti to mark the season. Although she lived farther away from the lake than her friends, her house made up for it with a stunning view of a gorge.

The other three women were already gathered in the kitchen, nibbling on snacks that Libbie had crafted. She was always trying out new recipes and bringing her culinary experiments to cocktail club for consumption and feedback, a habit that Julie wholeheartedly supported.

"I can't tell you how happy I am that it's Friday," Kate said. "I really need to relax this weekend. It's been nonstop lately."

"You're preaching to the choir." Julie drummed her fingers on the counter, waiting for Libbie to finish making the first round of cocktails. It was Libbie's turn to act as bartender and she'd chosen gimlets as their first drink of the night.

"One of the new cats at the shelter delivered kittens today," Rebecca said. "It was touch and go for a bit, but they're all doing well."

As Libbie passed the first glass into Julie's eager hand, she glanced over Julie's shoulder. "Is Greg with you tonight?"

"He was in the car. Not sure where he is now." She suspected he went to the deck to admire the view of the gorge. It was too dark for her to see anything, but according to Greg, darkness was no obstacle for his apparitional eyesight.

"I can't get over your gift," Rebecca mused. "Do you think he'll haunt you forever?"

"I hope not, for your sake," Kate said. "As much I love Lucas, I wouldn't want him haunting me. Knowing him, he'd figure out how to operate the remote from beyond the grave so he could still fill the DVR with all his favorite shows. We don't need to save every episode of *Naked and Afraid*, thanks."

Julie laughed and told them about the apple, as well as her visit to see Lorraine.

"Wait, you can do a spell that brings him back?" Libbie finished crafting the fourth and final drink and joined them in the cozy living room.

"Not exactly," Julie said. "He'd just be…less transparent. It's not like he'll have working organs."

Kate smirked. "That's too bad—for both of you."

Rebecca sat cross-legged on the floor in front of her. "Are you going to do it?"

"Not yet. It only lasts for a short window of time, so we want to choose our moment carefully." Julie tasted mint in the cocktail. The drinks were always more interesting when Libbie was in charge of making them.

"What I wouldn't give for another day with my mom," Kate said wistfully.

"What have the ghosts wanted?" Libbie asked. She gave her glass a little shake to shift the ice. "Are they lost or confused?"

"No, not at all," Julie said. She told them about her experiences with Barbara and Rosie.

Kate swilled her cocktail. "Your new business cards can say Communications Specialist for the Other Side."

"I don't know how you could do that day after day. It was an emotional day with Rosie and Mollie and I wasn't even the one in contact with the ghost," Rebecca said. "I came back here afterward and hugged all the animals."

Julie surveyed the downstairs. "Where are they?" Usually they had animals underfoot all evening at Rebecca's house.

"They're upstairs repenting their naughty behavior," Rebecca said. "Somebody got into the laundry basket and now I need to buy more of those high-waisted underpants."

Libbie laughed. "I love that granny panties now have more appealing names like shapewear or high-rise undies," she said.

"I don't care what they're called," Julie said, "I'm just glad my muffin top no longer hangs over the edge of my underpants like gelatin trying to escape from the container."

Libbie shook her head in awe. "Did you ever imagine that this would be the asset that Inga left you in her will?"

"Definitely not." Julie paused, a memory stirring. "I still remember something Inga said to me that last night with her. When I told her she'd managed to squeeze twenty lives into one and that I hoped to live even half as much..." Julie's voice broke and she paused to regain her composure. "She said, don't worry, my dear. You will."

"Do you think she meant the ghosts?" Rebecca asked. "That somehow she knew the gift you'd receive?"

"I don't see how since the gift is specific to the person," Julie said. "Although she obviously knew something remarkable would happen to us."

"Speaking of remarkable things happening..." Rebecca paused for effect and slid a sly look at Julie. "What did you think of Ira's son?"

Julie stared at the bottom of her now-empty glass. "David?"

"Yes, David," Rebecca said with an amused smile. "I was slightly miffed that he didn't seem interested in me, but since I love you so much, it only lasted like two seconds."

Two pink patches formed on Julie's cheeks. "I'm sure you imagined it."

"Okay, we need full details," Kate said.

"There are no details," Julie said. "He's Ira's son and he happened to be at the apartment when we went to see Mollie."

"And I detected chemistry," Rebecca added. "Unfortunately, I had more chemistry with Ira than his son."

"Ooh. How dreamy were his eyes on a scale of Jude Law to Paul Newman?"

Julie froze at the sound of Greg's voice. "This is just girl talk. She's not serious."

Rebecca clamped a hand over her mouth. "Oops, sorry, Julie."

"Is Greg here?" Libbie asked.

"Assume I'm always here," Greg said. "What else do I have to do?"

Julie set her empty glass on the counter. "Privacy, please. This is cocktail club and you're not a member."

Greg held up his hands apologetically. "I'll get out of your hair. Have fun drinking and talking about boys. If things escalate to a naked pillow fight, though, I reserve the right to return."

"Is he gone?" Libbie asked, surveying the room.

"For now." The heat in Julie's cheeks morphed into a full-blown hot flash and she shrugged off her extra layer.

"David is a doctor and *very* handsome," Rebecca said.

"Greg is also very handsome and he's excellent at playing doctor," Julie said.

Libbie snorted. "I just remembered how bad I was at that game Operation."

"It takes a very steady hand," Rebecca chimed in, remembering the game's tagline. "I bet you'd be good at it now. You're an expert with knives."

"I think my kids have Operation." Kate drank the rest of her cocktail. "We should bring it to the next meeting and see who wins after a few rounds of cocktails."

"Pretty sure we'd kill every patient on the table," Rebecca said.

At the mention of patients dying, Julie grew quiet, thinking of Rosie.

"Who's ready for another drink?" Libbie asked.

Julie raised her hand. "One more for me and that's it." She

leaned both palms flat on the counter. "While you're mixing, there's something else I'd like to talk about."

Kate looked at her curiously. "Do tell."

"I've been thinking about what to do with the rest of my life..."

"Gee, no pressure," Libbie murmured.

"And I've decided to convert my house into a bed and breakfast." Julie watched her friends' faces to gauge their reactions.

"You want to run your own business?" Kate asked.

A knot formed in Julie's stomach. "Do you think it's a bad idea?"

"I think it's an amazing idea," Libbie said, filling the cocktail shaker.

"I want to keep the house and a B&B seems like the best way to do it."

"Will you advertise as a haunted inn?" Libbie asked. "Have Greg slam a few doors. Relocate some shoes."

"That's not a bad idea," Julie said. "I'll need to keep him occupied somehow."

"The haunted angle would definitely attract guests," Rebecca said. "That place we went to in Salem is booked a year in advance."

Julie couldn't imagine her house being *that* in demand, although she had a feeling Greg would enjoy his mischievous role.

"Are you sure you want to run it as a B&B?" Kate asked. "That means you'd be responsible for breakfast."

"On that note..." Julie swiveled toward Libbie. "I was thinking of asking you to cater breakfasts for me." She cringed. "Does that sound crazy?"

Libbie stopped shaking and poured the drinks. "You want to hire me?"

Julie's head bobbed up and down. "I don't mind making an occasional meal for people, but it's never going to be my strong suit. Maybe we could work something out where you handle breakfast when I have a certain number of guests."

"That's a great idea," Kate said. "I love the idea of you two working together."

"Me, too," Libbie joined in. "And steady business is preferable to constantly drumming up clients. It's like running on a hamster wheel."

Julie clapped her hands, feeling more upbeat than she had in ages. "This is awesome. I'll let you know when I have more information. I'm just getting started, of course, and still need to figure out red tape."

"You should talk to Ethan," Libbie said, passing Julie a fresh cocktail. "He can probably guide you in the right direction."

"I was thinking of making an appointment with him," Julie said. "I'm kind of waiting for things with Brad to get resolved first."

"Is he still screaming bloody murder about the will?" Kate asked.

Julie took a drink. "He hasn't waved a white flag, that's for sure, and Greg saw him researching how to contest a will. As long as he's a threat, I'm afraid to make a real start on the business."

"Well, he can't stop you from gathering information," Libbie said. "Meet with Ethan and learn as much as you can."

"And show Brad you're tougher than he remembers," Kate added.

Was she? Julie wasn't so certain. "I don't know why he cares so much. He hasn't lived here in forever. He didn't give a rat's ass about our mom or me until there was a way for him to profit."

"That's who he is," Kate said. "He'll never change."

"If he's not going to change, then I wish he would leave."

Libbie slid cocktails across the counter to Kate and Rebecca. "Was he ever a good brother?" Libbie asked.

Julie held the glass to her lips, contemplating the question. "He wasn't someone who took responsibility. If there was a game and he lost, he would cry foul and blame someone else. A sore loser in every respect."

"Seems like he's continued down that path in adulthood," Kate surmised.

"Pretty much. I don't know anything about his current life, but it's obviously not very good or he'd have no reason to hang around here now and make my life difficult."

"I'm always fascinated when siblings are raised in the same house but turn out so different from each other," Rebecca said. "It's like a psychological experiment."

"I, for one, am excited about this B&B idea," Kate said. "I'll mention your place on my YouTube channel once you're up and running."

"Free advertising? Yes, please," Julie said.

"Whatever you do," Libbie said, "make sure your lake view is on every piece of marketing. On your website, too. That view is what's going to bring in the bodies."

"I totally agree," Rebecca chimed in. "I want to stay there for the view and I live locally."

"And emphasize your lake access, too," Kate said. "Your guests will be able to walk straight out the back door and into the water if they choose."

"Yes. I definitely want kayaks and canoes on the property for guests to use," Julie said.

"Talk to the marina," Kate told her. "They can give you all the information on boat rentals. You can have a binder with contact details in each bedroom."

"That's a great idea," Julie said. Her enthusiasm began to build as they generated more suggestions. It would cost money, of course, but, so far, nothing seemed insurmountable.

"This is going to be fun," Rebecca enthused. "I'm excited for you, but I'm excited to be a part of it, too."

Kate nodded. "Same."

"Inga would be so proud of you," Libbie said.

Julie warmed at the mention of their friend. "I don't know. I don't do nearly enough tequila shots to make her proud."

Kate wiggled her eyebrows. "That can be easily remedied."

Julie waved her hands. "Oh, no. Not tonight. I have way too much on my plate right now and I can't afford a hangover."

And if she didn't find a way to earn money soon, she wouldn't be able to afford anything at all.

THIRTEEN

Julie stood on the beach and admired the lake. A few professional photographs at sunrise and sunset and she'd have all the marketing materials she needed. Libbie was right. She'd book a visit to a place like this in a heartbeat based on the view alone.

She looked around the property and tried to envision where she'd store the kayaks and other water-based items. They had to stay close enough to the water for ease of launching, at least in the summer months. She pictured families staying in the house and enjoying all that Lake Cloverleaf had to offer. She'd try to negotiate a discount for her guests with local establishments like Pebbles and Cone Hut, the ice cream shop owned by Libbie's ex-husband, Nick. Julie liked the idea of supporting other local businesses. Maybe she'd even join the Chamber of Commerce like Libbie. Julie felt a surge of optimism. Fifty didn't have to mean that all change was bad. This new horizon seemed...encouraging.

"This place is beautiful. I'm envious. As hard as I worked, I didn't end up with a view this spectacular."

Julie turned with a start. It took her a moment to place him, but she finally recognized him as the man in the suit from the grocery store.

"It's you again."

"Tom Bronsky."

Yes, Tom. He'd said that at the grocery store, not that she was fully engaged at the time. "It's nice to meet you, Tom. I'm Julie Duncan."

"I take it this means you won't run away from me this time."

She offered a sheepish smile. "Sorry about that. I didn't know what was happening. You were my first encounter."

"No worries. I decided to wait and try again another time." He motioned to the lake. "I had a boat called Sundancer. I used to go right past this place and wonder who lived here." He smiled. "Now I know."

She glanced over her shoulder at the sprawling house behind her. "This place has been in my family for generations. I'm trying to figure out how I can keep it now that my mother's passed."

"What does your mother think?"

Julie shrugged. "I don't know. She left the house without instructions."

"You can't see her ghost?"

"No." Julie didn't want to share just how grateful she was for that omission. The prospect of Doris as a ghost in the house was terrifying. "I guess not everyone's as lucky as you."

"I don't know about that," Tom said. "I think the ones without unfinished business are the lucky ones."

Julie slipped her hands into the pockets of her jacket to keep warm. "I guess that's why you're here."

"I hate to break it to you, but you're like a beacon for ghosts. I was the first, but I can guarantee I won't be the last."

Julie faced the lake as a cold wind blew back her hair. "I guess I'll have to get used to seeing dead people."

"I'm not here to haunt you," Tom said. "I just need an intermediary."

Julie stuck out a hand. "Communications Specialist to the Other Side at your service."

Tom chuckled. "I'd shake it if I could."

"You need to practice, apparently. If you focus your energy, you can learn to manipulate objects in this realm."

"I don't plan to stick around long enough to learn anything." He lifted his chin toward the house. "Do you have time to take a drive?"

"To where?"

"Not far. Elm Street. Number twenty-two. Will you come?" His eyes shone with such hope that Julie couldn't refuse even if she wanted to.

"Let me get my keys," she said.

The house on Elm Street reminded Julie of a modern mountain retreat—a log cabin style with all the amenities.

"Great house," Julie said.

"It is. I wish I'd visited more often."

"It's not yours?"

"No. My son lives here."

Julie exited the car. "What now? Do you want me to ring the bell?"

Tom hesitated. "I think I need a minute to prepare. Let's go around back first."

Julie shot him a curious look. "What's around back?"

"There's a deck with huge windows. I like to stand out there and watch them sometimes."

"Gee, that doesn't sound creepy at all," she joked. "Why not go in?" Greg didn't seem to have any trouble entering the house. Then again, he'd actually lived there so he had an attachment to the property.

"It doesn't feel right."

"Uncomfortable being an actual peeping Tom, huh?"

He didn't smile. "I wasn't very welcome when I was alive, so it doesn't seem right to invade their personal space when I'm dead."

They skirted the house and walked to the backyard. Once on the deck, Julie positioned herself behind a support beam. Tom inched closer to the glass and gazed through the window at the scene within. A man in his early thirties sat at a kitchen table opposite a baby in a high chair, spooning applesauce into her mouth.

Julie's heart melted. "That's your son?"

He nodded somberly. "Justin. And that's my granddaughter, Hailey."

"She's precious."

A sad smile touched his lips. "She looks like Justin at that age. Same dimple in the left cheek. Do you see it? My wife and I used to make a game of getting Justin to smile just so we could see that dimple." He slid his hands into his pockets and they watched together for another moment in companionable silence.

"Is he your only child?"

Tom nodded. "We lost a child after him. She was stillborn."

"I'm so sorry. What was her name?"

Tom turned to look at her. "Hailey." He returned his attention to the scene inside. "My wife must've told him. It's not the kind of thing I talked about."

"It must've been hard."

"Hard on my wife. Hard on the marriage. Thankfully, Justin was too young to remember any of it."

"He seems like a good dad," Julie said. Justin seemed to genuinely enjoy the mess his daughter was making with applesauce. Julie's parents wouldn't have had the patience for it. Her mother once gave away a beloved LEGO set because Julie left a single blue brick on the floor. There'd been no warning. No teachable moment. Only swift retribution.

"Yeah, I wasn't sure what to expect, but it's been a relief."

Julie cocked her head. "You didn't think he would make a good father?"

"What we don't repair we're doomed to repeat, right? Let's just say I wasn't a model father."

Julie was beginning to understand why Tom was here—and why he'd called upon her for help. "If you were such a terrible father, you wouldn't be here now, would you? You'd pass Go, collect your two hundreds dollar on the way to the Other Side, and never look back."

"I collected all the money I ever needed." Tom broke off, his emotions appearing to overwhelm him. "I had my own insurance brokerage firm. A car and a house that people envied. I worked nonstop for them, though."

Julie noticed that Justin wore a blue T-shirt and faded jeans. There was a pink stain on the shirt that looked like paint.

"I take it Justin didn't follow in your footsteps. Were you upset he didn't take over the family business?"

"No, not at all," Tom said. "I would've been disappointed if he had." He nodded toward the duo. "This is much better."

Hailey squealed and grabbed the end of the spoon with the applesauce, prompting a laugh from Justin.

"This is why we're here? You didn't spend enough quality time with Justin?"

"I have regrets," Tom admitted, "about the kind of father I was. I was in the office when I died. Heart attack." He shook his head. "If someone had told me that's how I'd go, I would've done a lot of things differently." He inclined his head toward the window. "Starting with Justin."

"Is your wife still alive? Have you seen her?"

Tom averted his gaze. "We didn't have the best marriage. It's one of the reasons I buried myself in work, to avoid addressing problems. I justified it by giving my family everything they needed. Nice vacations. Expensive clothes. But Justin was the one who paid the price."

"Why not get divorced?"

"Because my parents divorced when I was a kid and I didn't want to do that to Justin." He gave a rueful shake of his head. "But I ended up screwing up anyway. I didn't want a divorce, but I wasn't happy. I wasn't good at faking it either. I thought I was at the time, but hindsight is 20/20."

"Did your wife ever try to talk to you about the marriage?"

"She suggested counseling once or twice, but it wouldn't have mattered. I know it might sound strange, but I didn't enjoy her company."

"You must've enjoyed her company at some point if you married her."

He grunted. "I was young. We both were. We got married before we knew who we were. By the time I figured it out, we had a son."

Julie leaned against the beam. "What is it you want me to do?"

"Tell Justin I'm sorry. Don't tell him about the marriage part. I don't want him to think I'm blaming his mom for my crappy relationship with him."

"Then how do I explain it?"

Tom rubbed the back of his neck. "I'm not sure. Let's wing it."

Julie wasn't so sure about winging it, especially given she was about to tell a stranger that she was conversing with his estranged dead dad. Unfortunately, there wasn't a roadmap for this sort of thing.

They returned to the front of the house and Julie rang the bell. Her anxiety flared when Justin opened the door, balancing Hailey on his hip.

"Can I help you?" he asked.

Julie flashed a reassuring smile. She was going to sound like a lunatic no matter how nice her smile was, but it seemed better than not smiling at all.

"Hi, my name is Julie Duncan. I live not too far from here."

Justin's eyes flickered with concern. "Is your car broken down? I've got jumper cables, a patch kit for tires—you name it."

"No, no. I'm fine, thank you." She pursed her lips. "Can I come in for a minute?"

Justin tightened his grip on Hailey. "Who are you again?"

"Tell him you're from Lightning Insurance," Tom said.

"I'm from Lightning Insurance. I'm here to talk about your dad."

Justin's face registered surprise. "Oh, got it. Come on in." He backed away to give Julie room to pass. "You knew my dad?"

"Yes." Julie immediately warmed to the idea. This was preferable to telling him about Tom's ghost. "I worked for him."

"Then I guess you saw him more than I did." He walked to the kitchen at the back of the house and returned his daughter to the high chair. "Can I get you a drink?"

"No thanks. I won't take too much of your time. I only want to say I'm sorry for your loss."

Justin looked at her sideways. "Not much of a loss."

Ouch. "You lost your dad, Justin, and Hailey lost her grandfather."

"How did you know my daughter's name?"

"Your dad told me."

"Huh. I'm surprised he knew her name." Justin peeled a banana and mashed it on a plate with a spoon before offering it to Hailey.

"I lost my mom recently," Julie said. She hadn't been planning to talk about her own life, but it seemed like a natural thing to share. "We had a difficult relationship."

A half smile formed on Justin's lips. "Ah, then you understand."

Julie slid into the chair adjacent to him. "Your dad told me a lot about you."

"I find that hard to believe since he didn't really know a lot about me."

"And it's the biggest regret of his life," Julie said.

Justin pulled a face. "Fat chance. His biggest regret was not buying that vacation home in Maui he used to talk about. One more thing to convince his friends that his life was perfect. He cared about outward appearances way more than he cared about me."

"I'm sure it seemed that way, but it wasn't true," Julie said.

Tom bowed his head. "Tell him I love him and I'm sorry I didn't show him that when I was alive."

Julie cleared her throat, trying to think of a way to convey the sentiment without revealing her ability. "I know it might not have seemed like it, but he loved you very much. I know for a fact he regrets not spending more time with you."

Justin snorted. "How do you know that?"

"He told me," Julie said. "We talked a lot about our families...in the office. And Tom—your dad said his lack of a relationship with you was his biggest regret in life and that if he could do it all over again, he'd do things differently."

"Even if it meant less money?" Justin shook his head. "My dad loved his statement pieces. Expensive car. Big house on the lake. Peloton for Mom. The more he bought, the better man he was."

"He was coping with his own issues."

"Not coping is more like it," Justin said. "He had so many opportunities to be a better dad and he passed every single time. Soccer games. Art competitions. Even birthday parties. He'd pay for an elaborate party because God forbid he didn't keep up with the Joneses, but he missed most of them, stuck at the office or dealing with a work emergency." Justin used air quotes to empha-size 'work emergency.'

Tears glimmered in Tom's eyes. "Tell him I saw his poster—the one in the competition in sixth grade for fire safety. He won first prize for his grade and they invited the parents, but I worked late that evening. He thought I never showed up, but I did. A security guard let me in after-hours so I could see it. Had to pay him twenty bucks, but it was worth it." He smiled. "You should have seen it. Even then, the boy had talent. All the other artwork had burning houses and fire trucks. Amateurs." He blew a raspberry. "My son's was literally a work of art."

Julie wondered why Tom had never told Justin before. It seemed that Tom had stored everything inside his emotional vault and now—now Julie was the key.

"Your dad told me about your fire safety poster in sixth grade," she said.

Justin perked up. "How did he remember that? I took first place. Won a gift card to a frozen yogurt place that isn't there anymore." His smile quickly faded. "Oh, did he tell you how he was supposed to show up to see it on display, but he was too busy?"

"He went, Justin. He saw the poster. He paid a security guard twenty bucks to let him in after-hours so he could see it."

Justin's brow furrowed. "Is that true?"

Tom edged closer to the table. "Tell him second place was meant to be a fire truck, but it looked like a rectangle on fire."

Julie repeated the statement and Justin smiled at the description. "Yeah, they were all pretty lame." He watched Hailey devour the last of the banana. "Why didn't he ever tell me that?"

Julie cut a quick glance at Tom.

"I don't know," Tom said. "I wasn't very good at self-reflection and I was horrible with communication. I didn't even acknowledge things to myself, let alone anyone else." He hovered close to Justin, as though the close physical distance would somehow make up for the emotional distance.

"Your dad didn't mean to keep you at arm's length," Julie said.

Tom lowered his gaze. "In hindsight, I can see that I let my inner demons do the driving instead of taking control of the wheel myself. I was a fool to let that happen."

Julie felt a rush of sympathy for the older man. Unfortunately, he'd learned his life lessons too little too late. At least Julie could do something to help him now.

"Your dad knew he wasn't very good with communication," Julie said. "And he didn't take time to analyze his behavior."

"No, he sucked at self-awareness. My husband thinks Dad was afraid of what he might find inside if he looked too hard."

Tom's shoulders sagged. "Justin deserved better from me."

"He wanted to give you a good life," Julie said. "A happy upbringing. He didn't have that himself, so I get the impression he didn't quite know how to provide that for you."

Justin smiled. "Evan said the same thing, that Dad did the best he could with the limited tools he had. My grandparents died when I was a kid, so I didn't know them, and Dad didn't have much to say about them." He wiped the baby's mouth with a cloth. "He didn't talk much about anything, really. Only superficial things. I don't hate him or anything. I've made a point of working through my issues over the years so I don't repeat them with my own children." He leaned forward and bopped Hailey on the nose. "I'm going to be a good daddy to you, little one. That's a promise."

Julie had no doubt that was true. It seemed that Justin was willing to do the internal work that Tom had avoided during his lifetime.

Julie looked at Tom to see whether he was satisfied with her intervention. The older man was too busy watching Hailey to notice. Julie noticed a faint smile on his lips. Yes, he seemed satisfied.

"I don't want to take up any more of your time," Julie said. "I just thought you'd want to know. My relationship with my mom wasn't the best, and if she'd confided in someone about me..." Julie's words caught in her throat. She didn't expect to feel so emotional. This was Tom's journey, not hers. "Anyway, I'd like it very much if they told me."

Justin unsnapped the baby's food-stained bib. "I appreciate you coming here. It's good to know my dad had more feelings than he let on."

"It was nice meeting you," Julie said, rising to her feet. "Best of luck with Hailey, but I don't think you'll need it."

Justin moved to escort her to the door, but Julie waved him off. "Don't go to any trouble. You've got your hands full. I can show myself out."

She started to walk toward the front door and realized Tom wasn't following her. She turned to see him lingering next to Justin and Hailey, wearing a serene expression. She slowed her steps to give him another minute with his family. Julie hoped he felt better now that he'd had the chance to unburden himself. When she finally reached the front door, she turned around to signal to him, but only Justin and Hailey were at the table now.

The man in the suit had vanished.

FOURTEEN

Julie arrived home, feeling emotionally drained after her visit with Tom's son. As she passed the living room, she did a double take. The curio cabinet had been stripped of its knickknacks, including the collection of ceramic cherubs and cardinals.

Would Brad have snuck in while she was gone and taken them to sell on eBay? It seemed unlikely, although she *was* still waiting on the locksmith.

"Greg?" she called.

Her ghostly husband appeared in the foyer. "You rang, ghost whisperer?"

She gestured to the empty curio cabinet. "Are you responsible for that?"

He grinned. "I thought you'd be pleased. I know how much those figurines annoyed you."

"How?" she blurted.

He wiggled his fingers. "I've been practicing. Not much else to do when you're gone."

Julie felt a pang of guilt. In helping Tom with quality time with his loved one, she was losing quality time with her own. Maybe she should try to stay home as much as possible, although that meant her life wouldn't be that different from when Doris was alive. Still, it was better to be home with Greg's ghost than be out in the world without him.

"At first I thought Brad had broken in and stolen them," she said.

"Fat baby angel chance," Greg said. "Now that I know I can move dozens of figurines, I'd be more than happy to deal with him if he dares to show his face here again."

Julie suppressed a smile. "I can just imagine his reaction to being pelted by a legion of fat baby angels."

Greg's expression darkened. "He'd blame you. Even if your hands were tied behind your back, he'd claim it was you."

Julie hated to admit he was right. Brad had myopic vision when it came to her. "I'm going to make tea and process everything I learned today."

"I'll watch, unless you want me to try to move the kettle."

"That seems like a recipe for disaster." She busied herself in the kitchen, filling the kettle with water and turning on the burner. "It was quite a day. I helped another ghost cross over."

"Look at you go," Greg said.

"His name was Tom. He needed me to communicate with his son. The guy had a lot of regrets." She shook her head sadly.

"I'm glad I don't feel that way," Greg said. "It helps to live life knowing it's only temporary."

Julie squinted at him. "If you don't have any regrets, why do you think you're here?"

"Your guess is as good as mine."

"The other ghosts seem to know what they need. I help them get it and they cross over." She folded her arms and studied him. "But if you don't need anything, then why are you here?"

"Because I'm awesome?"

She broke into a broad smile. "Well, there is that." She sighed. "I guess I shouldn't look a gift horse in the mouth."

He leaned his forehead against hers—sort of. "Any more thoughts about when we should try our Cinderella spell?"

"Soon. First, I'd like to get started on the paperwork for the

B&B. Kate and Libbie suggested that I create a business plan and I feel like I should have a first draft when I meet with Ethan tomorrow."

"I can help with that."

She laughed. "When have you ever drafted a business plan?"

"I guess you didn't go through my computer files after I died." He paused. "That's probably for the best."

"I didn't find your porn collection, if that's what you're worried about." The kettle whistled and she turned off the burner.

"Where is my computer?"

"In our bedroom closet. I wasn't sure what to do with it."

"Let's fire it up. I'll show you my secrets."

His secrets. Her husband had harbored secrets during their marriage. Julie couldn't disguise her surprise.

"Did I say something wrong?" Greg asked.

She poured the hot water into the mug and tossed in a teabag. "No, I just can't believe you hid an entire business from me."

"There was no business. It was an idea."

"An idea that you believed in enough to draft a plan." She marched upstairs and into the bedroom, rummaging through the closet until she found the laptop.

"Jelly, how can you be mad about this? I'm dead."

She whirled toward him with the laptop clutched in her hands. "I can be mad. Death doesn't stop feelings." She realized that truer words had never been spoken. "I'm mad at my mom and she's dead, too."

Greg followed her to the outlet where she plugged in the laptop and set it on the bedside table. She perched on the edge of the bed and frowned.

"Password?"

He wore a lopsided smile. "You can't guess?"

She typed in their initials followed by their anniversary date and the screen changed to a background image of Julie sunning herself on a raft in the lake.

"God, if only I'd known how thin I actually was then," she breathed. "I regret all the time I wasted thinking I was too fat."

"You've always been stunning."

She scrutinized the image. "Look at my hair. Why did you let me have my photo taken?"

"Obviously I'm a big fan or I wouldn't have made it my wallpaper."

She looked up at him and smiled.

"Open the folder called Future Me," he said.

She clicked and opened Finder, scanning the folder names. "What else am I going to find in the folder for Future You?"

"Nothing I wouldn't want you to see or we wouldn't be sitting here now."

"That's a relief." She clicked open the folder and saw a document entitled 'Business Plan,' as well as research articles and an Excel spreadsheet. The business was called Afloat and involved the rental of kayaks and canoes. She reviewed the contents, including the spreadsheet data.

"Greg, this is incredibly thorough."

He drifted over to sit beside her on the bed. "You sound surprised."

"Only that I didn't know about it. Why did you never share this with me before?"

"Because you were so busy with your mom and then with me." He averted his gaze. "At a certain point, it became clear it wasn't meant to be."

Julie continued to study the business plan. "You were serious about this."

"Why not? We have lakefront property and plenty of space. We would've needed zoning permission, of course, and I wasn't sure about your mom."

Her spirits lifted. "Greg, this is so helpful for what I want to do now." She turned back to the computer screen. "And there's no way my mother ever would've consented to strangers traipsing across her yard to get to the water."

"No, I'm sure you're right. That was one of the reasons it was in the future folder."

"I've been thinking about having kayaks and canoes to launch from here as part of the B&B's business, so your work wasn't in vain."

Greg placed a wispy kiss on her cheek. "I'm sorry I never got the chance to show you when I was alive. I guess I was worried that you'd reject the idea."

"You're sharing it with me now," she said, feeling grateful to have this second chance with her husband. "And it couldn't have come at a better time." She drummed her fingers on the table. "While we're one the subject, are there any other secrets you feel the need to divulge? Maybe an unhealthy obsession with Princess Leia's gold bikini."

He grinned. "That one's not much of a secret."

"True." She'd sat through enough viewings of Star Wars movies to know Greg's feelings about Princess Leia in all her outfits. "Thank you for sharing this with me now."

"What time is your meeting with the lawyer?" Greg asked.

"Ten thirty tomorrow."

"Are you going to ask him about Brad, too?"

"I have the appointment. I might as well get as much information out of him as I can."

Julie was so nervous about her meeting with Ethan that she changed her outfit three times.

"This is an appointment for legal advice and not a date, right?" Greg asked. "I'm just checking."

She smiled. "He's Libbie's boyfriend. I want to make a good impression and show him I'm serious about starting my business."

Greg's mouth twitched. "And nothing says serious like purple eyeshadow."

Julie's fingers flew to her eyelids. "Oh, God. It looks awful, doesn't it?" She rubbed off the powder with her fingers. "How about the clothes? Too casual?" For her third outfit, she'd chosen a white blouse with capped sleeves and black trousers.

"You look like you're either going undercover in a penguin sting operation or you're about to serve me a mini quiche."

She glared at him. "That's not helpful."

"Take a selfie and send it your friends for their opinion. Isn't that what the womenfolk do these days?"

"I don't want them to know I'm nervous. They'll think it's silly."

He pointed to himself. "No, *I* think it's silly. They'll be supportive."

"Forget it. I don't have time now. I need to go or I'll be late."

"Nothing says professional businesswoman like being late," Greg said, hurrying behind her.

"Again—not helping!"

Julie ignored him and grabbed her purse and keys. "Wish me luck."

"You don't want me to come with you? You said Ethan was Inga's lawyer, right? That means he knows all about your magical assets."

Julie stopped at the front door and turned to look at him. "I appreciate the offer, but I think I'd like to do this on my own."

As Julie waited in the reception area, she reviewed the list of questions for Ethan that she'd written in the Notes app on her phone. She had a tendency to get lost in conversation and forget the rest of what she wanted to say, so having a list written down in advance was a necessity.

"Hey, there. Julie, right?"

Julie was so engrossed in her notes that she barely registered the greeting. "Huh?" She glanced up at the handsome face of Ira's son and blinked rapidly. "David, what a surprise."

He inclined his head toward the office door. "Ethan's your lawyer, too?"

"He is now. He's dating a good friend of mine and I happen to be in need of legal advice."

"I hope it's nothing bad," he said. "A divorce, maybe?"

"Oh, I'm not married," Julie said. "Well, I'm a widow."

David's face fell. "I'm so sorry. That's even worse." He cringed. "I shouldn't have asked. Your meeting is none of my business. You would think I'd be more mindful of that given my own doctor-patient confidentiality rules."

"It's fine," Julie said. She was actually touched by how nervous he seemed. It was sweet and not at all typical for Julie. Greg had been a pretty confident guy, even when they'd first started dating.

"I had paperwork updated for my dad," David said. He raked a hand through his hair. "I'm oversharing, aren't I? It's a bad habit. My father warned me away from poker at a young age."

Ethan appeared framed in the doorway of his office. "I didn't realize you two know each other."

"We only met the other day," Julie said.

"It was great to see you again so soon," David said. He lingered for a moment as though he wanted to say more, but seemed to change his mind. "Take care, Julie."

Ethan motioned for Julie to join him in the office. "David's a great guy," he said, closing the door behind them. "Great doctor, too. I've known him for years."

"I met him at his father's apartment. His dad seems sweet."

Ethan relaxed in his chair and gave her a long look. "How are you, Julie? I mean really."

Julie clasped her hands in her lap. "I'm good."

"You lost your mom. You can't be that good."

She managed a smile. "I'm planning for the future and that helps keep my mind occupied."

Ethan offered an easygoing smile. "I'm glad you trust me enough to help you out."

"If Inga and Libbie trust you, then I trust you. I have a few things I'd like to address today. Now that my mom has passed, I'll need to update my will since she left me the bulk of her estate."

"That's simple enough. You also mentioned something about a new business venture."

"Yes, but before we get to that, I also need to talk to you about my brother."

Ethan nodded solemnly. "Libbie mentioned he's been giving you a hard time. I didn't want to bring it up unless you did."

"Is there any chance he can successfully contest my mother's will?" she asked. "I want to start the process of converting the house to a B&B, but I don't want to end up buried in litigation while I'm trying to get a new business off the ground. Now that I've pissed off Brad, all bets are off."

"*You* didn't piss off your brother, Julie. Just because he doesn't like the contents of your mother's will doesn't make it your fault."

Still, Julie couldn't help feeling responsible when she was the one benefitting from the decision. Where else would Brad direct his anger? Their mother was dead now. She was the only target left.

"He thinks he deserves half of the estate, but knowing him, he'll try to take all of it. He's throwing around terms like undue influence and researching how to contest a will."

Ethan made a noise of disapproval. "What's his situation? Does he have the money to hire a lawyer?"

"He has the twenty thousand dollars my mom left him—or he will, once the will has been through probate."

Ethan grimaced. "That's unfortunate. Do you think he'd want to spend it on legal fees?"

"I guess it depends on whether he finds a lawyer who takes his claim seriously."

Ethan nodded. "Unfortunately, there are plenty of unscrupulous lawyers out there willing to take cases they shouldn't."

"It puts me in a quandary because I'd like to get the house up and running as a bed and breakfast as soon as possible—I need the income—but I'm afraid to do anything official until I'm sure Brad will leave me alone. I have no idea how to handle this."

"I see your conundrum." Ethan fiddled with a shiny silver pen.

"I'd advise you not to hold up your plans for the house. If you want to make the business a reality, then start the process so you're ready to move once the will has been through probate. If your brother's going to take action, it makes sense for him to do it sooner rather than later."

Julie thought he made a good point. "What do you think his chances are of winning?"

"Based on what I know, pretty slim. Your mother was of sound mind and that's the key."

Julie released the breath she'd been holding. "Then let's hope he decides to spend his money on something else." He could spend it on beer for all she cared, as long as she got to keep the house.

"Now that we've gotten your brother out of the way, let's talk about something more positive, like your new business venture."

Julie felt a rise of excitement. "Yes. I've been doing a lot of research and I've been working on my business plan."

"Any questions so far?"

She laughed. "How much time do you have?"

He leaned back against the black swivel chair. "As much time as you need."

"What can you tell me about local zoning regulations?"

He smiled. "Now you're speaking my language." He spent the next half an hour explaining the process as Julie took notes on her phone. She didn't want to forget a single word.

"Your business plan looks good so far," Ethan said, after reviewing the document. "You'll need the final version if you plan to apply for a loan or an extension of credit."

"If I decide to make any renovations, I will. I don't have a lot of savings."

"Libbie had to apply for a loan when she decided to expand her business. You should ask her about it."

She vaguely recalled her friend mentioning it a couple months ago. "Thanks, I definitely will."

By the time Julie left Ethan's office, she felt excited about the path ahead. No matter what happened, she had a solid idea, a lawyer she trusted, and friends willing to help, and those facts boosted her confidence immensely. She couldn't wait to get home and share everything she learned with Greg.

FIFTEEN

Julie practically skipped into the house after her meeting with Ethan. She was starting to see the B&B as a tangible goal instead of a pipe dream. Even better, it was a project that was entirely her own. She would make all the decisions. The business would be an expression of her style and ideas. There would be no one lording over her, telling her she was going about it the wrong way or that the business was destined to fail. And even if the B&B did end up a flop, she would be proud for forging ahead and trying something new. For believing in herself.

"You look like a girl who just got the promposal of her dreams," Greg said, hovering in front of the fireplace.

Julie tossed her purse onto the counter. "What's the deal with promposals anyway?" She was glad they weren't a fad when she was in high school. The whole idea seemed regressive and unnecessarily expensive. "In our day, the money was spent on the tickets, the clothes, and the flowers. Maybe a limo if somebody's parents had money. Now even asking for a date costs money. It's ridiculous."

"Wow." Greg chuckled. "You've become the sort of person who says 'in our day.'"

"I know, but it's true. When someone spends that much money and energy on a proposal, it makes a girl feel compelled to say yes even if she doesn't want to." Especially a high school girl who hasn't yet developed a backbone. Julie was fifty and still developing hers, although she felt like she'd made a few strides of late.

"Well, I'm sure glad you said yes to my proposal." He spread his arms wide. "In fact, it was right here in this room. Do you remember?"

She ambled toward him, still feeling upbeat about her meeting. "On that note, why don't we take a look at Lorraine's spell and see what's involved?"

Greg cocked his head. "Are you sure? I'm guessing the lawyer gave you a list a mile long of things you need to do. I don't mind waiting."

"He did, but it was a good meeting. I'm starting to feel confident that this can work." She relayed the details of her meeting with Ethan. "I also ran into someone I met the other day. Remember I told you about the man who was looking after Rosie's dog?"

"Ira was at the lawyer's office?"

"No, his son, David."

Greg batted his eyelashes. "Oh, David. The dreamy doctor."

She waved a dismissive hand. "Stop. It's not like that."

"Maybe it should be."

Julie gave him a quizzical look. "What do you mean?"

"Maybe it's a sign from the universe."

Julie barked a laugh. "Our love was written in the stars? When did you start believing in fate?"

Greg splayed his hands. "Since I came back to you as a ghost."

Julie observed him in silence. There was no way the universe was interested in her love life and, even if it was, the fact that Greg was here now suggested he was the only one meant for her.

"David is a perfectly nice man, but as long as you're still in the picture, I am a very married woman."

Uncertainty flickered across his features and Julie wasn't sure how to interpret it. Did he think she wanted to go out with David? She was so engrossed in their discussion that she failed to hear Brad enter the house until he was standing in the kitchen.

Greg put a finger to her lips. "Um, Julie." He pointed over her shoulder and Julie craned her neck to see Brad staring at her intently.

"What are you doing?" her brother asked.

Julie's cheeks grew flushed. Her phone was on the kitchen counter so she couldn't pretend to be talking to someone.

"Nothing," she said. "What are you doing here? I've asked you before to knock before you come in."

Brad ignored her rebuke. "What's wrong with you?"

"Nothing." And just like that her positive outlook dissipated.

He pointed to the fireplace. "You were talking like someone's there."

"No, I wasn't." What else could she say? She was conversing with the ghost of her dead husband?

Brad narrowed his eyes. "There's nothing wrong with my hearing, Jules. I heard you talking about someone named David. Is that your imaginary boyfriend?"

"I was on speakerphone," she lied.

He cut a sideways glance at the island. "Your phone is all the way over here."

Julie changed gears. "Why are you here, Brad?"

"I was planning to tell you that I'm going to take my twenty grand and go home. Apparently, if I contest the will during probate, that holds up the whole proceedings and I'll have to wait until it's settled to get the money."

She tried not to let her relief show. "When are you leaving town?"

Brad hesitated. "I said I was *planning* to tell you, but now I'm not so sure."

An uneasy feeling crept through her. "There's no point in

fighting it, Brad. I spoke with my lawyer and he said your chances of successfully contesting the will are slim to none."

Brad scowled. "You talked to a lawyer about me?"

"I didn't go specifically to discuss you. I wanted advice about starting the B&B, which I fully intend to do."

"Here's the thing, sis. After what I just saw, I don't know that you're mentally competent enough to take care of this house on your own."

She folded her arms. "Good thing it's not up to you then."

His eyes glimmered with malice. "Might be if a judge decides you need someone to look after your affairs, like that pop singer did."

Julie's harsh laughter followed. "You think I need a conservatorship like Britney Spears?"

"If you're talking to walls and acting like they talk back, then yeah—a judge might decide you're mentally incompetent and need someone to look after you—and your *estate*, of course."

Greg moved into the kitchen and Julie sensed his temper flaring. She didn't want him to do anything that would push Brad further toward a conservatorship.

"You'd keep the house, like you wanted," Brad continued, "but I'd be your guardian. Make all the decisions." He glanced around the house, satisfied. "Basically, I'd run the place."

"I'm going to kill this guy," Greg seethed.

Julie kept her focus on her brother to avoid saying or doing anything out of the ordinary.

"That's ridiculous, Brad. It would be a complete waste of time and money," she said.

"Oh, I don't know." He paced the length of the kitchen, musing aloud. "You've been so depressed ever since your husband died. And then Mom." He swiveled toward her with a loathsome smile. "It's no wonder you cracked. Now you're seeing things. Talking to people who aren't there. There are places that specialize in this sort of thing. They might even prescribe medication to make those pesky visions go away."

Julie's blood ran cold. Was he threatening to have her medicated against her will or worse—committed? "Don't be an idiot, Brad. Take your twenty grand and leave me alone."

"I have big plans for this house, Jules. You have no idea. As soon as I got the news about dear Doris, I started to think about all the possibilities." He spun to face her. "But then you went and ruined everything."

"I didn't ruin anything," she said quietly.

"Sure you did, but we can fix that."

"I'd like you to leave," Julie said. "Now." Her whole body was shaking now and she wished she'd continued to call around for a locksmith until one was immediately available. "And please don't come back."

Brad lingered in the kitchen, as though debating whether to stay and harass her further. Finally, he made a move toward the door and Julie's shoulders relaxed.

"I'll make sure he goes and lock the door behind him," Greg said.

Julie wanted to comment on his advanced poltergeist skills, but it wasn't the right time. She was too emotionally overwhelmed to speak. Hugging herself, she sank onto the sofa.

"No judge is going to have you declared incompetent, Julie," Greg said. "He has no proof."

"What if he finds out about the people I've helped? I told Barbara's husband that I could see his dead wife. What if he tells someone and it gets back to Brad? He could use it against me." Julie drew her knees to her chest and began to rock.

"That's not going to happen," Greg said firmly. He drifted over to join her on the sofa.

"At least I didn't take the straightforward approach with everyone," she said. She'd told Tom's son she worked for the insurance company and she'd lied to Ira, too. Although Ethan knew about her magical assets, now that she'd hired him as her lawyer, he was bound by lawyer-client confidentiality and couldn't reveal what he knew.

"Your friends would rally behind you," Greg said. "They'd lie about your gift if they had to."

Julie cringed. She'd never want her friends to perjure themselves for her. She couldn't let things get that far.

"I do think I should lay low until this blows over," Greg said.

"I don't want you to lay low."

"We don't want to give him any ammunition against you. Knowing him, he'd set up secret cameras and record you talking to me."

"I'm changing the locks so he can't get in," Julie said stubbornly. "I don't want him to interfere in our lives."

"In *your* life, Julie. Mine is over, remember?"

Julie tilted her head. "You've always encouraged me to stand up for myself and now it seems like you want me to work myself into a pretzel to avoid his wrath."

Greg tried to stroke her hair. "Julie, you have to admit this could be bad for you. Your brother is a determined prick. If he finds you talking to a ghost—any ghost—he'll use it against you. I certainly don't want to be the reason you lose everything. I've hurt you enough."

"You haven't hurt me. Please don't think that for one second."

"Julie, I have caused you more pain than any one person has a right to inflict." His eyes softened. "I thought being here was a good thing, but I'm starting to think maybe this was a cosmic error."

Her heart skipped a beat. "Don't say that. You belong here—with me."

Greg averted his gaze and said nothing.

"What's your plan then? You hide indefinitely? Stalk the downtown area and gather gossip? We have no clue when Brad will give up and leave town. I don't want to miss out on time with you just because he's an idiot."

"It'll be until he calms down and lets go of this idea. Once he talks to a lawyer and realizes a conservatorship is a dead end, he'll stop lurking."

Julie balled her hands into fists. "The other day you asked me why I was crying when I left Barbara's house."

"I assumed it was because you wanted to keep the baseball," he teased.

She smiled. "Yes, you know me. Huge Phillies fan." She drew a deep breath. "Barbara wanted her husband to move forward. Adam was stuck in the grief stage and she told him to ask out the blonde who lived down the street."

"Ah, I see."

She bit her lip, dreading her next question. "Do you think I'm stuck in the grief stage?"

"I think you've been stuck somewhere," Greg agreed. "I'm not sure if it's the grief stage, although I'm sure my death didn't help."

Her brow furrowed. "What does that mean?"

"It means that you've been stuck in this cycle of powerlessness that probably started when you were a kid."

Julie shifted uncomfortably. "Is this about us or is this about my mom?"

"It's about everything. The whole kit and caboodle. The circus and all its monkeys."

She couldn't resist a smile. "I get the picture."

"You've felt powerless your whole life, which is no big shock considering your mother's domineering behavior. This is why Brad is able to get to you. He knows the buttons to push."

Julie blinked rapidly. "I'm sorry. Are you blaming *me* for the way my brother treats me?"

"No, no. Don't misunderstand me."

Julie inched backward on the sofa. "Maybe you're right. Maybe you should lay low for a few days until we know what he plans to do next."

Greg floated to an upright position. "I think it's the right call. I need time to think."

"Think? You're a ghost. How much thinking do you need to do?"

He ignored the question. "It's easier when you're not in the room," he said. "When you're in front of me like this...I just want to make our time together last forever, but it isn't fair to you."

"Once Brad is gone," she said. "Then we can be together."

He gave her a long look. "I'll see you again soon, Jelly."

Her spirits deflated, she continued to sit with her arms wrapped around her knees and stare at the empty space where her husband had been.

SIXTEEN

Julie kept herself busy with projects over the next couple days. Every task she tackled was a positive step toward her future. She called another locksmith to change the locks, tweaked her business plan, and received estimates for bathroom renovations. She would need to upgrade the existing bathrooms and add new ones to the remaining guest rooms. She had a list of items to discuss with Greg when he returned, but it had been radio silence for days. In fact, Julie hadn't interacted with any ghosts and she started to wonder whether her gift had an expiration date. Maybe not all magical assets lasted until death.

"These changes don't all need to be made at once," Mr. Porter advised. The heavyset bald man was the third of three contractors she'd called for an estimate. "I'd suggest you take it slowly and see how the business progresses. Have two rooms ready for guests and then decide whether you need a third. You can always have the work done during your off-season so it doesn't upset your guests."

Julie wouldn't know what her off-season was until she'd been up and running for a couple years. She'd have to ask some of the other proprietors in town and see whether there was a consensus across the board.

"You've given me a lot to think about," she said. They'd

returned to the kitchen from upstairs and Julie offered him a drink, which he declined.

"I've got another appointment right after this," he said. "It's January. Everybody has new goals for the year." He patted his stomach. "My renovation goals are limited to this. I'm laying off the sweets for good this year, I swear it."

Julie smiled. She knew that goal all too well. "Thank you so much for coming out."

"I'll get you a written estimate by the end of the week." He shook her hand. "It was nice meeting you. You've got yourself a great house. I'd consider it a privilege to do work here."

Her phone vibrated on the counter.

"I'll get out of your hair so you can get that." Mr. Porter tucked his clipboard under his arm and headed for the front door.

Julie didn't recognize the number on the screen and let the call go to voicemail. She opened the Notes app and started typing the results of her conversation with the contractor. She knew better than to try to remember the details later. Her brain was Swiss cheese at this point and she needed to make things easier on herself. She was pleased with Mr. Porter's visit and decided he'd be best for the job. Once she received the written estimate, she'd finish her business plan and make an appointment with a loan officer. Things were looking up.

The sound of the front door caught her attention. "Did you forget something, Mr. Porter?"

She glanced at the counters but didn't see anything left behind. It was possible he'd left a measuring tape upstairs in one of the bathrooms.

"Mr. Porter?" Her smile dissolved when her brother appeared at the far end of the kitchen.

"How's it going, Jules?" He staggered forward a few steps and nearly tripped over Peggy. The cat shot into the family room to avoid a collision.

"What are you doing here?" Julie demanded. "I told you not to come in without knocking."

"Your boyfriend let me in." Brad seemed slightly unsteady on his feet and Julie suspected he'd overindulged at the bar.

"Mr. Porter is a contractor," she said.

He raised his eyebrows. "Oh, for the work you plan to do to *my* house?" he asked, and promptly belched.

"I think we've already established this is not your house, nor will it ever be." Anger rose within her. How dare he disrespect her again? She'd made her position and her feelings crystal clear, yet still he chose to violate her boundaries. Enough was enough.

He swaggered toward her with a menacing glint in his eye. "Do you really think you can take what's mine? You don't have the guts." He wagged a finger at her. "You're the one who made this harder than it had to be. You could've just given me half but noooo. You had to be selfish and greedy. Typical woman."

Every muscle in her body tensed. "Get out, Brad," Julie said. "Leave now and stop embarrassing yourself."

Brad scowled. "Make me."

Calmly, Julie picked up her phone. "How about I have the police make you? Does that work for you?"

Brad clenched his hands into fists. "I wouldn't do that if I were you, little sister."

Julie sensed there was a reason he didn't want the police involved. That fact didn't surprise her. "Then I suggest you do as I ask and leave. I don't care if you grew up here. This isn't your home now and it never will be again."

He leaned against the wall and his mouth twisted into a lazy smile. "Mind if I smoke?" Without waiting for her response, he retrieved a pack of cigarettes from his back pocket.

"As a matter of fact, I do," she said.

Ignoring her, he pulled out a packet of matches.

"Leave now," she said, "and don't you dare light a cigarette in this house." Julie hated the stench of cigarette smoke, but even more than that, it seemed disrespectful to their mother's memory.

Brad's gaze flicked to the stovetop behind her and his lip curled into a smirk. Julie's heart stopped when his intention registered.

She couldn't quite believe it. He would rather burn down the house with her in it before letting her have it. Could he really be that vindictive?

She held up the phone. "Brad, I will call the police right now and tell them what you're threatening to do. If anything happens, they'll know it was you."

He ran his tongue over his top lip. "Not if I get to you first. You never were very fast."

All the air seemed to leave her lungs. "Brad, listen to yourself. You sound like a crazy person."

He shrugged. "I guess it runs in the family. At least I'm not delusional."

A month ago, his words would've stung, but now they held no weight. They were simply air. No matter how difficult it was, she had to face the awful truth. Her brother was a monster.

"This is your last chance. Leave now and don't ever come back."

His mouth twitched. "Nope," he said, making a popping sound with the 'p.'

Positioning herself between her brother and the oven, Julie tapped the screen to call the police. Unfortunately, Brad was right —she wasn't fast enough. He sprang forward and knocked the phone from her hand before she could finish the call. Julie staggered backward and fell on her backside. Pain radiated from her tailbone and she struggled to return to her feet as a cramp spread from her calf to her foot. She watched in horror as Brad turned on the gas burner. He struck a match and held up the flame, taunting her.

"You realize you can't run fast enough to escape," Julie said through gritted teeth. The pain from the cramp was paralyzing and she tamped down the desire to cry out. She didn't want Brad to see her as weak because Julie didn't feel weak—not anymore.

"I'll outrun you, I know that much." He flicked his wrist, preparing to toss the match. Before he could release it, a gust of wind blew through the room and extinguished the flame.

Julie lumbered to her feet and stretched her leg to get rid of the cramp. There was another presence in the room, but it wasn't Greg. She glanced around wildly for the source of the wind.

"I told you there was a draft in this stupid house. We're gonna need old Porter to take care of that." Brad tugged the packet of matches from his pocket. Before he could light another one, the knob of the stovetop turned off and the glow of the gas disappeared. The movement didn't escape Brad's notice.

He looked accusingly at Julie. "What just happened?"

"The burner's off."

"No shit. Is it broken or something?"

"Or something." She hobbled closer to retrieve her phone, but he knocked it aside before she reached it.

He tried to light another match and the flame blew out the moment he struck the match. He glowered at Julie.

"What in the hell do you think you're doing?"

"I'm not doing anything," she said.

A pan rose from the sink and smacked Brad in the cheek. He stumbled to the side as the pan dropped to the floor and caught his foot. He tripped and fell against the counter, cursing at Julie with every breath.

Part of her felt nervous because she had no idea who was attacking Brad, but she was also confident the spirit meant her no harm. She couldn't explain it—she just *knew*.

Julie scooped the pan off the floor and gripped the handle with both hands. "Get out of my house now or you're going to regret it." She pulled the pan over her shoulder and held it in a ready position.

Brad regained his balance and staggered toward Julie. The tap turned on and the nozzle sprayed water directly in her brother's face. Brad squeezed his eyes shut and fought his way to the sink to turn off the tap. When he turned back toward Julie, his foot slipped on the wet floor and he fell backward, hitting his head on the edge of the counter on the way down.

Julie lowered the pan and peered over the island to check on him.

"The idiot's unconscious, but I don't know for how long."

Julie's breath caught in her throat and she turned to see her mother standing in the kitchen. Doris wore her favorite peach-colored terrycloth robe and stood without the assistance of a cane.

"Mom?" she croaked.

"I can't believe it," her mother said.

"I know. I never would've believed it was possible until I saw my first ghost." Somehow it didn't surprise her that her mother would be the kind of ghost to arrive with advanced poltergeist skills.

Her mother made a dismissive noise. "Not that. I mean you. You stood up to your brother. It was like watching that chubby boy in Harry Potter stand up to his friends."

Julie rolled her eyes. "His name is Neville, Mom, not 'that chubby boy.'"

"Who cares? You get the idea." Doris drifted closer to observe her son. "This is my fault. I created this mess."

Julie felt a pang of sympathy for her mother. "You can't blame yourself. No one exists in a vacuum. Brad's an adult who makes his own choices, just as I make mine." Julie didn't have to take care of her mother or put up with her domineering personality for all these years. She chose to. Even if it was out of familial obligation, the choice had been hers and she didn't regret it. She only regretted not learning to stand up for herself sooner.

"I think you should call the police and tell them what happened. Well, tell them most of it. You don't want to end up in a padded cell."

Julie was shocked. "Are you sure?"

"Your brother's a menace to society. Why do you think I kept him away from us all these years?"

Julie frowned. "You kept him away? I thought he stayed away because..." Well, she didn't know why.

"It was for the best, trust me. I didn't want him anywhere near you. He was difficult to control and he never did the right thing, even when the choice was obvious." She clucked her tongue. "I did what I could for him, but it was never enough."

"He came back because of the twenty thousand dollars."

She heaved a sigh. "I debated whether to leave him anything at all, but maternal guilt got the better of me, I suppose. It felt cruel to cut him out completely." She glanced at the packet of matches on the floor. "I can't believe he had the nerve to try to smoke in this house after all I went through to quit."

Julie didn't care about the cigarettes or the matches. Right now, she wanted to talk to her mother. "How did you end up coming back here?"

Doris's gaze swept the room. "I don't know. One minute I wasn't aware of anything and the next minute, I had an overwhelming urge to come to you."

"Because you sensed I was in danger?"

Doris blinked in confusion. "No, because I left without saying..." She trailed off and glanced out the window with a dazed expression.

"Goodbye?" Julie prompted.

Doris turned back to face her. "I love you."

Julie's throat thickened with emotion and she couldn't seem to form words.

"I'm sorry I was so hard on you," her mother continued. "You were good to me, better than I deserved. I should've been grateful for you, but instead I took you for granted." She shook her head. "I was such a broken person inside and I lashed out at you because I knew you were the one person who'd never leave me."

Julie tried to process her mother's admission. "I'm sorry you were hurting. I wish I could've helped you."

Her mother's face radiated tenderness. "Believe me, you did. More than you know."

"I wish we could start over."

Her mother shook her head ruefully. "You have no idea how much I wish that, but what's done is done, though I'm particularly sorry about the way I handled Greg's death. I was a beast and I know I made your pain worse. It was unforgivable."

"You did your best," Julie said. Her mother had always lacked compassion and Julie could hardly have expected her to change overnight just because Greg died.

"I know it doesn't seem like it, but I was worried about you. I thought if I distracted you enough, that you wouldn't be sad all the time, but it didn't work." She paused. "I see now that was my mistake. I should've let you be sad and maybe the feelings would've passed instead of taking root."

But the sadness had taken root, burying itself so deep inside Julie that she could no longer access it. It seeped into the marrow of her bones and became a permanent part of her.

"I don't blame you for any of it," Julie said. Her mother's behavior stemmed from her own upbringing. Julie knew she'd had two parents more interested in each other than their children. Her mother reacted by being the opposite kind of parent—overly involved and controlling.

Julie reached for her mother's hands and they slid right through the air. "If it makes any difference to you, I forgive you, Mom."

"Don't just forgive me that easily because you're weak..."

"No," Julie interrupted. "Not because I'm weak. Because I'm strong. I love you, Mom, and I forgive you."

As mother and daughter stared at each other for a protracted moment, Julie understood that this was the reason her mother had returned—that Julie was her unfinished business.

Not anymore.

"There's something I wanted to ask you," Julie said. "It's silly, but I found a box of pennies in your closet."

Her mother clutched her chest. "The pennies. I'd completely forgotten about them."

"Dare I ask why you kept a shoebox full of pennies?"

Her mother pressed her hands against her cheeks, remembering. "Because they reminded me of your father. He liked to keep pennies in his pockets so that he could jingle them. After he died, every time I found a penny, I'd pick it up and keep it. It was my way of remembering him."

Julie's chest ached at the revelation. Her mother had been more sentimental than Julie realized. "Thank you for your help with Brad. I'd better call the police before he wakes up." Julie picked up the phone and called the police, as well as the paramedics. After all, Barbara died from a similar fall. As upset as Julie was with her brother, she wasn't prepared to let him die.

"You should get a restraining order, just to be on the safe side," her mother said, "although I have a feeling that, once he sleeps off this headache, he'll never want to come back to this town again."

"And what about you?" Julie asked. "I didn't expect you to come back. I've been making big plans for the house. Fair warning—changes are afoot."

Doris surveyed the downstairs. "Good. It's about time. This place is long past due for a makeover."

"Really?" Julie wasn't planning to ask for her mother's blessing, but she was pleased to have it regardless.

"You've got my head on your shoulders and your father's heart," Doris said. "You were the best of both of us and I know whatever you choose to do next, it's going to be amazing." With a ghostly hand, she managed to move a wispy strand of hair off Julie's forehead. "I'm proud of you, Julie. You've grown into an amazing woman."

The sound of an approaching siren spurred her into action.

"You'll be even more amazed when you see my business plan," Julie said. "Let me show you really quick before the police get here. You're going to be so impressed." She whipped toward the kitchen table to retrieve her laptop. "I've got forecasts and data and..." She spun around to share the screen with her mother, but the kitchen was empty.

With a heavy heart, Julie set the laptop on the counter and closed the lid.

"Goodbye, Mom. Rest in peace."

SEVENTEEN

Julie was shocked when she awoke at nine the next morning. Somehow she'd slept for a full eight hours, which hadn't happened in years, not since her insomnia started. She'd spent the remainder of yesterday at Kate's house, updating her friends on Brad's arrest and her mother's unexpected appearance. They'd been shocked by Brad's actions, and actually shrieked when Julie told them about her mother's intervention.

"Was she wearing her peach robe?" Libbie had asked.

Julie had laughed. "As a matter of fact, she was." Julie hadn't told them that the peach robe was the only article of her mother's clothing she'd kept. It was hanging at the back of Julie's closet and she'd opted not to wash it so that she could still smell her mother's disgusting perfume when she was in the mood to reminisce.

She rolled out of bed and showered, mulling over the tasks for the day. There were no appointments or meetings, so she thought she might head to the marina and gather information from the boat rental companies. It was nice to have the freedom to operate on her own schedule, without worrying about hurrying home to take care of someone else.

She wandered downstairs in lounge pants paired with one of

Greg's old T-shirts and her hair still damp from the shower. Peggy trailed behind her, meowing desperately for food.

"I'm sorry," Julie said. "I swear I won't make a habit of sleeping in." Okay, so she still had Peggy to take care of. Julie didn't mind. As far as Julie was concerned, Peggy gave a lot more than the cat received.

Julie arrived in the kitchen to find Greg waiting for her. She stopped short and peered at him. "You're back." Part of her had wondered whether he'd disappeared like the other ghosts. The fact that he hadn't suggested he still had unfinished business to address.

"I am." He glided over to her. "I'm sorry we had a moment."

"Same. You're going to be disappointed, too. You missed all the excitement." She told him about Brad and her mother.

Greg's eyes widened. "Wow. You weren't kidding about excitement. I'm sorry I wasn't here, but it sounds like you handled it."

"Well, I had a little help from Mom, but yeah. I handled it."

Greg took another minute to process the update. "Why does it not surprise me she was able to throw around a frying pan?"

Julie shrugged. "That's my mom."

"Now that Brad's out of the picture, what would you think of doing the spell today?"

Julie looked at him with a start. "The one from Lorraine?"

"Is there another one you're keeping a secret?"

She laughed. "No, that's the only one."

"Your brother's gone. No new ghosts have cropped up for handholding. You've made good progress with the B&B." Greg opened his arms wide. "I think it's our time, Jelly."

The prospect of touching Greg again sparked joy in her heart and she bustled over to her purse to find the written instructions for the spell. "Lorraine said the spell might last six to eight hours, but she wasn't sure. That would give us the whole day together."

"And then I'll turn into a pumpkin?" he teased.

"And then you'll be incorporeal again."

He gazed at her. "God, I hope it works. It would be so nice to hold you again."

Julie felt exactly the same.

She gathered the ingredients she'd brought home from Lorraine's shop and produced a mortar and pestle from the pantry. She slipped on her reading glasses for a better view of the instructions. Like Lorraine warned, she didn't want to deviate and make a costly mistake.

"This is oddly sexy, watching you toil away," Greg said. "You're much hotter than those other witches."

"My friends?"

"I was thinking more along the lines of Snow White's stepmom." He pondered the question. "Or the one with the candy house in the woods."

Julie wiggled her hips from side to side as she pushed on the pestle. "You like what you see, huh?"

"I like everything about you, Julie Duncan."

She finished grinding the mixture and then set it aflame. The smoke wafted through the air and she opened the back door to make sure she didn't set off the smoke detector. She didn't want to explain this concoction to the fire department.

Julie waved the magic smoke in Greg's direction and watched him intently for any sign of change. The ghost shimmered for a brief moment before the color returned to his flesh and his form hardened.

Greg stared at one arm and then the other. "I can't believe it. It's a miracle."

Julie lunged at him and looped her arms around his neck. "It's magic!" She kissed him fiercely and her spirits soared when she felt the weight of his body against hers.

They broke apart and looked at each other with wide smiles.

Greg flexed a bicep. "Should I do anything manly while I'm in this condition? Want me to take out the trash or climb a ladder to change a lightbulb?"

"I'm used to doing that on my own now."

He wrapped a hand around her waist and squeezed. "Can I cop a feel of those boobs now?"

She gave him a playful swat. "Seriously? You die and that's the first thing you want to do when you're back in a body?"

He wore a sheepish expression. "I can't help it. I haven't gotten laid in two and a half years."

"Neither have I."

He glanced down at his jeans. "Unfortunately, I don't think that's going to change today. No blood flow or functioning organs." He scratched his chin. "Does this make me a zombie? An animated corpse?"

Julie pressed her cheek against him and breathed in his scent. "I don't mind what you are. Whatever it is, it's enough for me."

"I guess this is the physical embodiment of my spirit." Greg pressed his lips against hers. "Zombie sounds cooler, though."

"You're a ridiculous man, Greg Duncan, and I love you to pieces." She bounced on the balls of her feet, vibrating with excitement. "What should we do today? Wrap up warm and walk around downtown? Lunch at Pebbles? They brought back that shrimp appetizer you loved so much."

Greg gave her a mournful look. "We can't do any of those things, Julie. We can't leave the house and risk anyone seeing me." He tapped his stomach. "Not to mention the fact that I can't ingest anything."

Julie was undeterred. "We could take a ride in the car. Drive through the mountains. Go for a hike." She glanced at his feet. "Except I gave away your boots and sneakers."

He curled his fingers around hers and brushed his lips across her knuckles. "You should call that doctor, David, and invite him for a hike," Greg said. "He sounds terrific."

Julie's brow furrowed. "I think I'm otherwise engaged."

"I don't mean today. I mean...after."

"After what?"

Greg released her hands and took a step backward. "We can't continue like this. It's not a life for you. By all accounts, David's a good guy with a sweet dad he dotes on. Why not give him a chance?"

"I don't need David when I have you."

Greg winced. "Yeah, about that."

Julie searched his face for answers. "What?"

"I told you I was going to think while I was gone."

"And?"

"And it's time," he said.

Julie shot a quizzical glance at the clock on her phone. "No, it isn't. We have hours before the spell is broken."

Greg offered a sympathetic smile. "I think you know what I mean."

Julie gripped his arm. "No, you can't leave. You only just got here."

Gently, he removed her fingers that were pressing into his flesh. "It's not going to get any better than this. Today is the pinnacle."

She shook her head adamantly. "No, I'll just keep doing the spell over and over. We can have as much time as we want."

"I don't think it works that way, Jelly. It seems like a one-shot deal."

In her heart of hearts, Julie knew he was right, but she didn't want to believe it. She wanted more—more time, more physical contact, more Greg.

"Remember how we wondered why those other ghosts needed your help, but I didn't?" He cupped his hand under her chin. "I think it's because *I* was brought back to help *you*, not the other way around."

"So keep helping me."

"You're ready, Julie," he assured her. "You don't need me anymore."

"Of course I need you. How can you say that?"

"There's a difference between need and want," he said quietly. "You're strong enough to handle whatever comes your way."

"I'm not. I'm a mess. There'll be more obstacles to overcome."

He kissed her forehead. "And you will tackle each one with

grace and humor because that's who you are. Besides, as long as you have your memories, I'll always be with you."

Tears pricked Julie's eyes. She wanted more than memories. She wanted him in the flesh. She wanted to grow old together and laugh at their respective ailments. She wanted…

Want. Not need.

She wiped the tears that striped her cheeks. Greg was right. She *was* strong enough to stand on her own two feet. She'd found her voice and she was no longer afraid to use it.

He clasped her hands in his and held them against his chest. "Believe me, if I could stay, I would. There's nowhere I'd rather be than with you, but not like this." He glanced down at himself. "You've been chained to this house for years. If I try to cling to my old life here, you'd be my prisoner and I don't want that for you. You deserve so much more than that."

Julie nodded through a veil of tears. "I don't want to spend this time arguing with you."

He kissed her forehead. "Then don't."

They spent the next few hours setting aside the inevitable and pretending it was a normal day. She updated him on her progress with the B&B and he made suggestions for the business plan and they talked about how Julie could integrate his ideas for the kayaks and canoes.

Afterward, they sat on the bed together and flipped through their wedding album, laughing over Greg's drunken uncle who tried to sing a Celine Dion song in the middle of the reception, and the school buses that turned up to transport their guests instead of the tasteful trolleys they'd hired.

She showed him the garish Christmas suit that she kept in the closet. He offered to don it one last time, but Julie refused. She wanted the last memory of him wearing the suit to be an authentic one—their last Christmas together before he died. It had been a bright spot in an otherwise miserable year.

Occasionally, Julie would squeeze his arm to make sure he was still solid. The last time she checked, he grabbed her hand and kissed it.

"I love you," he said.

"I love you, too."

"Promise me you'll let go," he said. He kissed her tenderly on the lips.

"I promise." She would acknowledge the reality and then she would move on with her life the way she should've done the first time around.

"Good. Now let's spend our last few hours doing something fun."

"Let me make chicken parmesan," she said. "It won't take long."

He smiled. "You know I can't actually eat it."

"I know, but it will feel normal and I'll enjoy cooking your last meal."

"Just don't burn the pan," he teased.

"Hey, I'm only a little bit incompetent."

Julie vacated the bed and went downstairs to get started. She insisted that Greg relax at the table and talk to her about his day, as though he'd come home from a long day at work. When she struggled with the cheese grater, he tried to intervene, but she pushed him back to his chair and completed the task on her own.

They dined on the deck and Julie spent most of the meal peeling off her sweater and then putting it back on again. Greg seemed amused by the constant changes.

"You're lucky you're dead. My nose is getting frostbite out here."

"We can go inside whenever you want," he said.

"No, I want to be out here with you and enjoy the view." This was how she pictured their life together. Serene and content.

Greg admired the food on his plate. "It looks delicious."

"Tastes delicious, too," Julie said, shoveling another forkful into her mouth. She followed that bite with a mouthful of red wine.

"How would you feel about a movie?" he asked.

Julie met his gaze. "Are you sure?"

He reached across the table and brushed his thumb across her wrist. "I want to cuddle on the sofa in front of a roaring fire and watch a movie."

Julie burst into laughter. "Apparently, it takes death to get a man to cuddle."

His eyes shone with sincerity. "I want to hold you until the very end, Julie. Like in the hospital."

Julie cleared the emotions that clogged her throat. She remembered that day well. The foul smells of the hospital. Greg's weak arms. She'd hated every second of it and yet she never wanted it to end.

"Empire Strikes Back?" she asked.

He grinned. "You know me so well."

Julie cleared the table and left the dirty dishes in the sink. There'd be plenty of time to clean tomorrow. Today belonged to her husband.

They cuddled on the sofa with Julie's head resting on his shoulder.

"Call David," he said, in the middle of Yoda trying to train Luke to use the Force. "If not for yourself, then do it for me. I hate the thought of you living the rest of your life alone."

Julie sat up and looked at him. "If it would mean that much to you, then I'll call him."

Relief rippled across his features. "Do you promise?"

She crooked a pinky. "You want me to pinky swear?"

"I'm not saying you have to marry him or anything, but give him a chance. If you like him, great. If not, no harm done. It's a step in the right direction."

"You realize this is a strange conversation to be having with your wife."

"We've had a lot of strange conversations over the years, Julie. It's one of the reasons we had such a solid relationship. We could say anything to each other. You were my safe space and I was yours."

He was right. She settled back against him and tried to concentrate on the movie. She imagined the sound of his heart beating and pretended that this was a normal weekday night, like so many she'd taken for granted before. Her eyelids grew heavy and she kept sitting up with a start before falling asleep again.

"You make a comfortable pillow, Greg Duncan," she murmured. "Your dad bod has no equal."

"If I'd known I'd be stuck with this body in the afterlife, I would've taken better care of it when I was alive."

"You're the hottest guy I know, dead or alive. Han Solo doesn't hold a candle to you."

She heard his soft chuckle as she drifted off to sleep. Her dreams were complex and strange, with Julie wielding a light saber and cutting down Darth Vader. When he removed his helmet, Brad's face looked back at her.

"Forgive me," he said.

She threw down the light saber. "I already have."

When she awoke later, the room was dark and her head rested on the cushion. The television had returned to the Disney home screen. Slowly, Julie looked around the room for any sign of her husband.

"Greg?"

Peggy stood on the kitchen counter and meowed sadly, heralding the news Julie already knew.

Greg was gone.

EIGHTEEN

"Whose brilliant idea was this?" Rebecca complained. "It's below freezing and we're trekking up a mountain."

The four women were wrapped in heavy coats and knit hats as they hiked uphill in their boots.

"It was Greg's idea," Julie said, although her voice was muffled by the thick scarf she'd wrapped around her face to protect her from the wind. "Would you like to file a complaint with my dead husband?"

Rebecca scowled. "Oh, sure. Play the dead husband card. My legs are killing me, so I guess I'll be joining him soon. I'll tell him you said hello."

"Just think of that bottle of bubbly we get to open when we reach our destination," Libbie said.

Despite Rebecca's complaint, Julie seemed to be the only one panting. Now that the B&B plan was in motion, she was going to have to boost health and fitness to the top of her list of priorities.

"Look, there's a cardinal," Libbie said, pointing.

Julie followed her friend's gaze and spotted the red male perched on a tree branch. Seconds later, a female joined him. Julie observed the birds for a moment, thinking of her mother. It would be impossible to see a cardinal now and not remember her mom.

Julie decided this was one of the upsides of memories. She could choose to let them be painful, or she could choose to let them be comforting.

Julie chose to let the sight of the cardinals comfort her.

"I, for one, think you picked a great day for hiking," Kate said. She inhaled the fresh air. "Spring is just around the corner. I can sense it."

"I don't know how you can sense anything. Your nose hairs are like tiny icicles," Rebecca grumbled.

"And you're Lake Cloverleaf's very own groundhog," Julie said, smiling.

"And you're our very own ghost whisperer," Kate shot back. "How does it feel to be a messenger of the dead?"

"I prefer a voice of the spirit world," Julie said.

"You can offer seances at your B&B," Rebecca suggested. "That'll get people in the door."

Libbie ducked under a branch. "Too bad it's not still haunted. That would be a definite marketing angle."

"Less talking, more walking," Kate ordered. "I have a million things to do later."

"Speak for yourself," Libbie said. "I have a party to cater tomorrow and I need to prepare."

"And I have a date tomorrow," Julie said. "I guess I'll need a new outfit."

Her three friends halted in their tracks.

"Wait, what?" Rebecca gave her a gentle shove. "How could you wait until now to tell us?"

"Because it seems inappropriate to talk about it now when Greg's with us." Julie tilted her head to indicate the backpack she was carrying.

"Greg's the one who encouraged you to date," Libbie pointed out. "He'd be glad to know you took the plunge."

Julie's mind drifted back to her conversation with David. He'd sounded so shocked and delighted to hear from her. She had to admit, his response had been gratifying.

When they reached the overlook, Julie took a moment to stretch. She noticed how good she felt as she turned and twisted.

"Look at you," Kate said. "Day three of yoga and you're already making it a habit."

"You'll make a yogi out of me yet," Julie said. Fifty or not, it was never too late to initiate healthy habits.

Kate popped the cork off the bottle and filled four plastic flutes. The four women toasted to Greg, and Julie admired the view of the snow-capped mountains as she sipped her drink.

"Greg would love all this pomp and circumstance," Julie said, draining the flute. She unzipped the backpack she was carrying and removed the container with Greg's ashes. She held it against her chest and sighed. "Magic is truly the most amazing thing that's ever happened to me."

"Same," Kate and Libbie said in unison.

Because of magic, Greg was able to make her see how unhealthy it was to keep his ashes next to her bed. More importantly, he was able to tell her where he wanted his ashes scattered. It should've been the kind of thing they discussed when he was sick, but Julie tended to avoid the more somber topics because she didn't want anything to remind her of the loneliness ahead. Greg had tried on many occasions to talk to her about practicalities, but Julie would change the subject before anything was resolved—but not anymore.

"Inga gave us an incredible gift," Libbie said.

Julie sighed softly. "She really did."

"Not me," Rebecca said. "My assets seem to be in name only."

"Your turn will come," Kate said with her usual confidence. "Inga would never let you down."

Libbie slid an arm along Rebecca's shoulders. "Definitely not. She was one of us."

"I think it's actually that we're one of her," Kate said.

Julie removed the lid from the container. "I'm ready if you are."

"Music, maestro," Kate said.

Libbie tapped the button on her phone screen and the *Star Wars* theme song blasted at full volume.

"What is it you're supposed to say?" Rebecca asked. "To infinity and beyond?"

Kate laughed. "That's Buzz Lightyear."

"In my defense, it sounds like something you might want to say when you scatter a person's ashes," Rebecca said.

"Greg is...*was* a Star Wars fan," Julie said. She had to start thinking of him in the past tense again. It would be challenging, but she felt confident she could do it.

"Scatter his ashes, you will," Libbie said in her best Yoda voice.

Rebecca wrinkled her nose. "Okay, let's not do that again."

"May the Force be with you," Julie shouted as she released the ashes. They leaped from the container as though they had a life of their own, and she watched with satisfaction as a gust of wind rushed past and carried them away.

A LETTER FROM THE AUTHOR

Huge thanks for reading *Vintage Spirits*. I hope you were hooked on Julie's journey. If you want to join other readers in hearing all about my new releases and bonus content, you can sign up for my newsletter!

www.stormpublishing.co/annabel-chase

If you enjoyed this book and could spare a few moments to leave a review that would be hugely appreciated. Even a short review can make all the difference in encouraging a reader to discover my books for the first time. Thank you so much!

Thanks again for being part of this amazing journey with me and I hope you'll stay in touch – I have so many more stories and ideas to entertain you with!

Annabel Chase x

www.annabelchase.com

facebook.com/annabelchasewriter

x.com/AuthorAnnabel

instagram.com/annabelchaseauthor

www.ingramcontent.com/pod-product-compliance
Lightning Source LLC
Chambersburg PA
CBHW011600190726
48287CB00010B/2979